[illegible]

Dear Mike —

I didn't write this — but I should have. I think you'll adore every word of this book. Love,

Josh

JOE & THE SHOW QUEEN

Larry Howard

Stamford, Connecticut

Published by Knights Press, P.O. Box 454, Pound Ridge, NY 10576

Distributed by Lyle Stuart, Inc., Secaucus, NJ

Cataloging-in-Publication Data

Howard, Larry.
Joe and the show queen / by Larry Howard.
p. cm.
ISBN 0-915175-30-4 : $9.00
I. Title.
PS3558.O88197J6 1989
813'.54—dc19 88-29257
CIP

Printed in the United States of America

For everyone who loves musicals

and for Richard, who hates them

JOE & THE SHOW QUEEN

ACT ONE

OVERTURE

"If life was meant to be a nonstop picnic," my grandmother used to say, "the cows would milk themselves." The day I walked out on Tony, the cows were waiting at the barn door. Our life together didn't seem like a picnic anymore, and a guy has to do what he has to do, whatever the consequences. At least that's what I told myself at the time. But a couple of hours later, copying phone numbers off a laundromat bulletin board and hoping the change machine wouldn't run out, I started having doubts. Tony or no Tony, the middle of a snowstorm in January wasn't the best time to give up a nice warm house on the lake.

Laundromats, at best, are not my favorite places. Sure, I've read how in big cities, New York, say, or San Francisco, guys meet each other cruising the Maytags. But this town isn't San Francisco, and the only action in the place was an argument between two fat ladies, in Spanish, over who was going to take the last drier. I've never understood why laundromats always have more washers than driers. But there are a lot of things I don't understand, and laundromats are easy compared to Tony.

Rooms are hard to come by in a college town, especially during the semester break when everyone with someplace better to go clears out. The first eight people I got through to all said the rooms were gone, and three of them even asked me to take down their signs. Since the snow was almost to the top of my Reeboks and still coming down hard, I knew I'd have to scramble if I was going to avoid crawling back to Tony with my tail between my legs. So I grabbed the gym bag I'd filled with a few essentials and, my socks squishing and my toes freezing, I made my way up to the campus. I was a desperate man.

Hidden away on the top floor of the union was the little cubby hole the gay students' alliance called an office. I crept past the open door maybe five, six times, hoping the guy at the desk would get busy doing something before he noticed me. When he finally disappeared behind a bookcase to answer the phone, I pulled up my collar and tiptoed in, one ear on that phone conversation and one eye on the door. I managed to jot down four or five numbers before the guy hung up, and I was out the door just as he asked if he could help me. I ran down to the lobby phone and grabbed a fistful of change from my pocket. The first couple of people I talked to said the rooms were gone, the next wanted a nonsmoking Christian woman, fem only, cat OK. The last guy gave me his address and said I could come right over to see the place.

I should have been relieved, but my resolve was weakening. Maybe this wasn't such a good idea. Sure, there are a lot of advantages to having a gay roommate, and it's not like I was in the closet — a year with Tony saw to that — but a guy can't be too careful, and here I was about to knock on some stranger's door in the hope of moving in with him. I guess I hadn't thought this far in advance when I slammed that other door, on Tony.

But I had no choice. Twenty minutes later I found myself squinting through the snow at an old brick house that had been divided up into four apartments. The location was good, midway between downtown, where I worked, and the campus, where I still sort of felt I belonged even though

I wasn't in school any more. This might not be so bad after all, provided the guy turned out to be — how can I put this? — not too obvious.

Halfway up the stairs the doubts set in again. Whoever opened that door was going to know where I'd gotten the number, and I didn't exactly make it a habit of announcing my sexuality to strangers. And what if he turned out not to be a stranger? If he was someone I knew? Maybe someone who'd recognize me from the store? Some old friend of Tony's? I had to remind myself none of this was likely. Since I'd dropped out of school I hardly ever ran into anyone I knew, and as for gay guys, I probably wouldn't recognize more than a few. Partly Tony's fault, partly my own. Like I said, I had to be careful. I glanced out the landing window and saw that the wind had picked up, so I took a deep breath and raised my hand. The door opened almost before I knocked.

"I was beginning to think you weren't coming." The guy was a few years older than me, maybe as old as twenty-eight or -nine. Tall and thin, ordinary face, ordinary brown hair, an ordinary looking guy. Better yet, I didn't recognize him. And he seemed, well, normal. At least so far. He waved his hand for me to come in and have a look around.

I had to admit the place was OK. Neat and clean with decent furniture, not like the student apartments I'd seen in this neighborhood, with ratty old second-hand chairs and peeling walls. These walls were painted and covered with colorful posters from old movies or something, I didn't pay much attention. But I did notice they were in frames, with glass, not torn and taped to the wall like Tony's muscle-man posters. Decorating was not one of Tony's interests. Musclemen, unfortunately, were.

"My name's Alec," the guy said, offering his hand. "You said on the phone your name's Joe?" I nodded and concentrated on his grip when I took his hand. You know what they say about judging a man by his handshake. My hands were so cold I couldn't feel a thing.

"Would you like something to warm you up? A cup of coffee? Tea?"

"I'm kind of in a hurry. Could I see the room?"

He turned around with a movement that was a little odd, not really a swish, more like a grand gesture. I'd been hoping he'd be butch, like me, and I decided I'd better watch him closely before I made up my mind. But the room was really nice — a good bed, the desk and dresser even matched. And the carpet was clean. No more of Tony's nail clippings greeting me when I reached down for my shoes.

"How much?" I asked him.

"Half the rent is one seventy-five a month, utilities included. Other arrangements will make it more."

"What other arrangements?"

"Why, food of course, glorious food. If you want to cook for yourself, you're on your own. If you want to go in together, we can split the groceries fifty-fifty, or you can give me a fixed amount and I'll see what I can do with it. I'm very creative. And what's more, baby, I can cook!"

The room *was* nice, but this "glorious" and "baby" stuff was definitely not what I was looking for. And he had this funny way of talking. Like that line about cooking. He'd raised his eyebrows and wiggled his shoulders and said it in a funny singsong way. Just as I was about to say no thanks, he got businesslike.

"There are a few things we have to get straight, if you'll pardon the expression. You got my number from the gay listing, so that's no secret. I'll respect your privacy and expect you to do the same in return. If my stereo's too loud, just tell me. You can trick if you must, but no lowlifes coming in here — I demand consideration and discretion. This is a nice house. I may be doing my Fräulein Schneider bit, but there's no Sally Bowles across the hall. Understood?

I caught the part about the stereo and discretion, but the rest of it kind of got by me. I was glad to see this guy at least had some backbone, but even so, I couldn't help thinking he was just a little wierd. "Can I give this some thought and call you back?"

"Go ahead, but you won't find anything better. That notice just went up on the bulletin board this morning. I didn't mean to scare you off, but I think some things should be clear from the start. I guess I sort of forgot myself. People don't always know what to make of me. It's a habit, the way I talk. But sometimes the title says it all — 'I've Gotta Be Me.' "

"Yeah, sure. Look, I'll let you know."

"OK. I wouldn't mind having you around." He narrowed his eyes and lowered his voice. " 'You're what a guy might call delish . . . packed as solid as a knish.' " Then, back to his regular self, "But I won't hold the room forever."

I didn't know what a knish was, but I could tell what he was thinking by the once-over he gave me. "Well, if I do take this room, don't get any ideas. Let's get *that* straight from the start, too." I didn't want to blow my chances before I'd made up my mind, so I eased off. "I'll let you know once I've decided. All right?"

"Anything you say." He opened the door for me. Then, his voice lowered, he repeated, "Anything you say."

Except that time he didn't *say* it. No, I was sure of it; the crazy guy had been *singing* to me. This was gonna take some thought.

SCENE I

Fade Out — Fade In

I stopped for a cup of coffee while I weighed my options. But I knew I didn't have any. Either I'd take that room and Alec with it or go crawling back to Tony. I could imagine how he'd act when he saw me, the way he'd lord it over me that I couldn't stay away, be cold and haughty until I'd apologized, like it had all been my fault. Then he'd start breathing on the back of my neck, knowing what *that* did to me. I supposed making up would be nice, it always was. But tomorrow, I knew tomorrow we'd have the same argument all over again.

Now this Alec, he was hardly my idea of a perfect roommate. He certainly wasn't my type, so skinny and lanky like a big bird, not into fitness like I am. Not that he was ugly or anything, there was just something about him. Something? There were lots of things — his exaggerated way of moving, those things he said that didn't make sense, his goddamn singing. I mean, this wasn't the sort of guy I'd want to be seen in public with, especially someplace like down at the store where people knew me. This was a guy who'd be likely to give himself away as soon as he opened his mouth. Now Tony, he was a different matter.

We were a great pair, Tony and I, him with his dark hair and Italian good looks, me with my blond hair and blue eyes. And our bodies, like bookends. Oh, Tony's biceps were bigger than mine, and he had thighs like oak trees, but my waist was smaller so I looked more built-up in the chest. Tony and I did everything together, running, working out. That is, until Tony decided that Nautilus wasn't fulfilling his potential. Then he started driving to the city to work out in a fancy gym. "What's wrong with the weights down at the club?" I asked him. "Why go all the way to the city?"

This other place, he said, had everything. Nautilus, Universal, a jacuzzi. And serious guys, power lifters who could show you the ropes. I knew he was going to try to convince me to go with him, but I didn't give him the chance. No way, I told him. Those Nautilus machines, they're safe, as long as you strap yourself in and use them right. But lifting weights, that can be dangerous. "Suit yourself," he said, "but you'll see, I'm going to have a fabulous bod." I thought he already did.

I'd really fallen for Tony. He had the kind of physique I'd always fantasized about, the kind you'd see in a magazine ad for underwear or deodorant and suddenly you'd find yourself locking the bathroom door. And what definition — biceps, triceps, deltoids — pecs you could break a plate over. He was my inspiration. We had a nice thing going, at least we did at the beginning.

Tony was a waiter in the fanciest restaurant in town. He had to wear a uniform, like a tux, with a frilly white shirt that he wore a size too small so that every move he made, you could see his chest straining against the material. He was a knockout in it, and he knew it. He also knew how to turn on the charm, so he made great tips. The hours weren't terrific, but I agreed to work Saturdays and a few nights down at the store so we had plenty of time together, especially since I'd always wait up for him. Then Tony started coming home a little later than usual, then a little later than that. Not all the time, but often enough that his excuses about trouble balancing the receipts didn't hold up. And he started flashing big bills. Tips, he told me, just tips. But I couldn't help wondering where that money was coming from. And where those late hours were going.

Of course I suspected he was seeing some other guy. He'd tell me I was the only man who ever mattered to him, but still, we had a couple of doozies of fights over his late nights. And just around the time he promised me he'd get home earlier, he started disappearing in the afternoons, between the lunch and dinner shifts. In the beginning, when I first moved in with him, he'd rush home for a quickie no matter how little time he had; toward the end I ticked off the hours watching soap operas while I got ticked off at Tony. Then I noticed his clothes started smelling of strange smells, smells I didn't recognize as Brut or Aramis or English Leather. So we had it out, once and for all.

"What's the big deal?" he complained. "You're giving me all this grief because of the way I smell? I stopped at the gym for an extra workout and shower."

"The soap at the gym doesn't smell like gardenias."

"I used a cake someone left behind."

"Bullshit."

"What do you know?"

"I know your membership expired two weeks ago, and they won't let you work out when you're expired."

He spilled his gut. Seems the fucker had been turning tricks. A lot of rich women came into that restaurant, career types who didn't have time to date but did have the money to pay for an Italian dessert. When the late nights got to be a hassle, he started doing matinees.

"They're just women," he said, "no big deal. An hour at lunchtime and they hand over the bread, no questions, no strings. I'm only doing it for us."

After every fight he'd give me some expensive present, a sweater or shirt I'd admired in a store window. Then he'd run his tongue around the inside of my ear, which he knew got to me even quicker than breathing on the back of my neck and which wasn't playing fair, but which did make it awfully hard to stay mad at him. So I put up with it as long as I could, giving in to his sweet talk and his ear-tonguing and not wanting to lose him.

Then he came home with a new scheme. Seems one of the women he was putting it to had connections in the city, a group of rich friends who wanted to open a male strip joint. Tony, of course, had already passed the first round of auditions. He thought this was the chance of a lifetime, and pretty soon he was going into the city on his nights off to prance around in a G-string while these horny dames shoved bills in his pouch. He loved it. Told me he was making so much money he didn't have to fuck for bucks anymore, and they were, after all, only women.

He loved it, all right. He even wanted me to start doing it, too. Now I may not be the small-town boy I once was, but some things just don't seem right, and prancing around in the almost-altogether while a bunch of heated-up women slobber in their Perrier is one of them. So faced with the choice of getting up there and doing it with him or keeping quiet while he did it himself, the second was the easy way out. But he wouldn't give up. He was always telling me these great ideas he'd dreamed up for our double act.

''We'd be dynamite together,'' he kept insisting. ''Think of the fun we'd have working up our routines.'' It seems you had to have a regular act, a gimmick, to get them warmed up. One guy'd come out dressed like a cop, another a soldier or construction worker, then they'd start to strip. Tony was working on this bit where he'd start out in a business suit, a hat, glasses, looking a little wimpy. He was supposed to be Clark Kent. Then he'd strip down to a Superman outfit underneath; that was supposed to be the real turn-on, watching Superman squirm out of his tights. He was really into this routine. "Sure is lucky I'm going to that new gym," he told me. "Gotta work out if I'm going to pull off Superman." Which made sense, I guess.

But when he started coming home from the the gym smelling of smells I knew *were* Brut and Aramis and English Leather, I knew Superman wasn't the only one he was pulling off. Turns out that gym had the busiest locker room this side of the Manhattan Y. That was when I came home with a box of condoms. I expected Tony to put up a fight and when he didn't, I knew things had gone further than he was willing to admit. So I told the man of steel he either limits his occupational pursuits to waiting tables, or I walk. "You wouldn't," he said with that smug look of his. "You *couldn't.*" He watched me pack like he was enjoying himself. "See you for supper, Joe. In the meantime, I've got important things to do." Oh, he had important things, all right. When I left he was trying to work out a way to paint a big red S on himself without getting it matted in his chest hair.

So that was how I ended up drinking coffee in a blizzard and coming to the conclusion that I'd have to trudge back through six inches of snow and take that room and the weird guy who went with it.

"But only until I find someplace else," I told him.

He just smiled and said in a funny, high-pitched voice that I should consider myself part of the furniture. Which struck me as odd, but what the hell, I knew I'd be out of there in a couple of weeks. Tony had a few erogenous zones of his own. He'd miss me.

Or so I thought. See, I'd always prided myself on my ability to size people up. And once I had, I figured that was it — people didn't change. At least that's what grandma said. Like when Mr. Perkins down at the drygoods store overcharged her a penny or two, she wasn't surprised. She'd go over her receipt item by item, then march right back into town to get what was due her. "Never could trust that man," she'd holler. My Dad once told me that old Mr. Perkins started overcharging her on purpose, just to have the satisfaction of knowing how much time she'd have to spend trying to pick up the error. "Son," he told me, "people get as good as they give. No better, no worse." Which turned out later to be a good lesson, but not one to convince grandma. She'd poke me with her bony finger and tell me, "You can wash a mule ten times over, and all you're doing is wasting soap. And that Claude Perkins is as set in his ways as any mule I ever met."

I used to believe grandma in most everything she said. But lately I've been having my doubts. People *do* change — because they have to, they want to, or they just wake up one morning and find that everything is so different from the way it was the day before that either they changed or the whole world did, and the latter wasn't too likely. And that's what happened to me. Back then, when all this started, I was pretty damned sure of myself. But this is one mule who got a good scrubbing — and came up smelling like a rose.

SCENE II

The Sound of Music

I spent the next few days getting my stuff moved in and put away. I had to time my trips back to the old place so as to avoid Tony. I was sure he had to be rethinking things, and I didn't want to see him while the memory of our last fight was still fresh in our minds. After I'd gotten all my clothes, I had no choice but to leave the key with a note telling him my new phone number, just in case he had to get hold of me. I found myself hanging around my room a lot, on the chance he'd call, and before I knew it a week and a half had gone by. Here it was a Saturday night, me all alone with nothing to do. What *could* I do? Sit in a movie surrounded by all those hand-holding couples? Hang around on campus and watch the nerds study? Go out for a drink? There was only one place in town that gay guys went to, and going in alone was not something I was ready for. At least not yet.

Even if I went to the bar, I couldn't show up before 10:30 or 11, so I still had a long night to fill, and besides, since I'd started working so hard on my body and gotten muscles and definition, there weren't many guys who really appealed to me. I used to be turned on by all sorts of men, but after you've been hanging around a gym, you get used to fantastic bodies, and ordinary guys just don't cut it any more. And as long as I'm on a truth kick here, the rock-bottom line is, I didn't have much experience in gay bars or in meeting guys. I didn't have any snappy opening lines or clever conversational gambits; I mean, if you're out of school you can't even fall back on talking about your classes. So I guess I was just a little nervous about being thrown into that scene. I stayed in my room that night, arranging my sweaters by color and hoping Alec would go out so I could have the run of the place, maybe watch some TV. I didn't have anything against the guy, other than that he was scrawny, not too butch, and a little odd, but since this was going to be a temporary living arrangement, I didn't want him to get any ideas about making me part of the furniture, which must be what he'd meant by the screwy remark.

I hadn't seen much of Alec, that first week and a half. Our work schedules didn't overlap, so we passed each other coming and going, and when we were both home, I stayed in my room. I didn't want him to think I was settling in — after all, Tony would be calling any day. If I didn't see much of Alec, I sure heard him a lot, playing his stereo at all hours. Once in a while I even recognized a song or two, and then I wouldn't bother to close my door all the way. Most of the time he sang along, and he seemed to know every word to every record by heart. Even when there was no music playing, he'd be singing. I guess he was just a cheerful guy.

That night, I wasn't in the mood for cheerful. I'd never minded being alone on a Saturday night before, even when Tony was late getting home, because waiting for him made the time pass. But I knew he wouldn't be turning up, and the night seemed endless, and I was really pissed at that bastard for lousing up a good thing.

About 7:30 Alec knocked on my door. "Are you hungry?" he asked, as it swung open.

"I thought I'd make a peanut butter sandwich or

something. I haven't had a chance to go shopping yet.'' He made a face. ''Peanut butter is pure protein, and I only get the natural kind, you know, that you have to stir. If you're going to grow muscle, you have to eat protein.'' Needless to say, I'd already told him I'd do my own cooking. The less I was involved with him, the better.

''Well,'' he said, ''I've got a quiche coming out of the oven and a salad, so you can join me if you want. Or don't men with muscles eat quiche?''

Now I knew all about quiche, because it was on the lunch menu at Tony's restaurant and once in a while he brought some home. And I had to admit it smelled awfully good. Why not, I figured, just this once.

As soon as I saw the table I knew I'd made a mistake. Alec had set it real fancy, with cloth napkins folded into some sort of flower or something, candles, and a bottle of wine. But the sight of that quiche cooling on the stove put thoughts of peanut butter out of my head, and since it would just be this one time. . . .

''How do you like the apartment?'' Alec asked me while he opened the wine.

''Fine. It's OK. But you know, I'm not planning to stay long.''

''Sure.'' He dished up the dinner and sat down. ''I didn't expect anyone to see my notice so fast, especially not in that storm. Why'd you leave your old place?''

''I, uh, had a disagreement with my roommate. He'll be calling to apologize any day now, so I'll probably be moving back.''

''Of course.'' He smiled. Which I didn't like, since he had this look like he was humoring me or something. OK, if that's how he wanted to play it.

''So what happenend to *your* last roommate, Alec?''

He pressed his hand to his heart in one of those gestures of his and looked up at the ceiling. ''Ah, Jason. A sweet young thing. But a little too young and not quite sweet enough. He was enamored of my anatomy, at least a certain part of it. Our love was deep — about eighteen inches between us. Not deep enough, I guess. Which is to say he subsequently and somewhat precipitously fell for a freshman he picked up in a campus tea room. We went from 'If Ever I Would Leave You' to 'So Long Dearie' faster than you could say 'Shipoopi.' "

Since I wasn't sure what he was talking about, except for the campus tea room, and the less said about that the better, I didn't answer him. Finally he asked me how the dinner was, and I said good, which was true. Then after we didn't say much else for a while, he sighed. Then he crooned at me. " 'I love a quiet girl.' "

That got to me. "You know, Alec, I really don't like it when you talk like that, I mean this 'baby' and 'girl' stuff. And the *way* you talk, I have a hard enough time following you without all the singing." I didn't want to sound *too* mad, since I was sitting there eating his dinner, but those were just the things that had me trying to avoid him. "What's with you, anyway?"

He threw up his hands. "Who can answer the musical question so aptly posed in the song, 'How D'Ya Talk to a Girl?' Sorry, it slipped out. A reflex. A lot of what I say comes from songs — everything reminds me of a song. You name it, I've got a song. See that, 'I've Got a Song,' that's another song title right there. *Bloomer Girl.*" The look on my face must have said it all. "You don't know what I'm talking about, do you?" He waved his hand around the room. "Haven't you noticed my posters?"

"They're OK. Colorful." I'd never taken a good look at them. They just seemed like a blur of pink and purple, like I'd said, colorful. I glanced over at the wall and took a closer look — peacock feathers and flowers, just what I'd expect with a guy like Alec. I shrugged and turned to him. "But I never heard of these movies."

"Movies!" He laughed out loud. "The day they make a movie of *Dear World* or *Hallelujah, Baby!*. . .Those are shows. Broadway shows. Haven't you ever seen a Broadway musical?"

"Sure. When I was in high school, the senior class put on *Oklahoma!* And I saw the movie of *Grease*. And when I was a kid my older sister used to listen to *Hair* all the time. She told me everyone got naked in it, but I didn't believe her. So that's what you're always listening to, musicals?"

He threw his hands out in front of him, shook his head and started to croak, " 'Broadway B-a-a-a-by-y-y.' Or," he said cheerfully, "I am, as some would put it, a Show Queen. I've got over 400 albums, some of the rarest. Tell me if there's one you want to hear. Even *Hair*, that damn spoiler."

"I kind of liked it. My sister said it was full of dirty words that I shouldn't be listening to, so I listened a lot closer. But I couldn't tell which were the dirty words. What did I know, I was just a kid. Don't you like it?"

"Oh, the music's good. But do you know what that show did? That damn album sold more copies than just about any musical up to that time. That's what that show did!"

"So?"

"It was the beginning of the end of Broadway, that's all. Suddenly everybody's doing rock musicals. All that amplification and electronic stuff. Name me a rock musical with one hummable melody. The beginning of the end." He jabbed his finger in the air. "Broadway used to supply this country with its popular music. Songs became hits before the shows even opened — first night audiences would applaud familiar tunes during the overture. Then rock came along. Instead of fighting it they started putting lousy rock into lousy shows. Where's the feeling? Where's the song that tells a story? No wonder the book musical died. String some songs together in a revue and name it best musical. Broadway lost its integrity, betrayed its own traditions. Rodgers and Hammerstein, Jerome Kern, they struggled for years to create the *integrated* musical.'' He threw his hands up. ''What do we get now? It's all staging, costume, glitz, *concept* shows. And it all started with *Hair!* Broadway lost touch with its audience.'' He snapped his fingers. ''Like that!''

He was really worked up. I wasn't too sure what to make of this guy, talk about your strange. I had the feeling he had a lot more opinions about Broadway shows, and if I was smart, I wouldn't mention one again. I'd rather hear him singing them than ranting about them. ''You know, Alec, you're weird.''

He smiled. ''It could have been worse. I might have been an Opera Queen running around the place singing *'Casta Diva'* and *'Vissi d'arte'* in Italian. Then you wouldn't understand *anything* I said.''

I'm not sure, but I think I might have preferred it.

I was feeling pretty full after Alec's dinner, so I never did go out that night. And the next night we ate the other half of the quiche and a fabulous strudel he'd spent half the day on. It was loaded with calories and all sorts of bad things, but runners need carbohydrates, and apples are good for the digestion, so I accepted a second piece. I was starting to think Alec wasn't really all that bad, as long as you stayed off the subject of musicals. He'd kind of scared me the night before, but now, leaning back with a good cup of coffee, I was feeling more at ease and decided to get some answers to questions that had been on my mind.

''Alec, how come you OK'd me to live here? I mean,

so fast? You didn't even ask me if I had a job. You should be careful about things like that."

"I usually am. But I knew who you were."

"You did?"

"You and your boyfriend, Tony, you were quite a couple around town. Parading your bods through all the fancy shops, jogging out there early in the morning. A lot of people were disappointed last fall when the weather turned cold and you two put on shirts and long pants instead of those cute little running shorts that barely covered your behinds."

I knew Tony and I were noticed, but we only wore those shorts because they were comfortable. "I can't help it if other people like to look."

"I used to watch you myself. From the front window. You'd pass by every morning around 7:30." He held his hands up over his head, twisted them like claws and began to chant, " 'Isn't that enough to make your. . .isn't that enough to make your day?' That was my Anthony Newley, in case you were wondering. So what happened between you two? Everyone said you were an ideal pair." He turned and sang to an empty chair. " 'They make a perfectly lovely couple, don't they? They do!' "

"I'd just as soon not go into it. Like I said, I expect him to call."

"Sure. Have some more strudel. And as for your income, I know you work in that sporting goods store down in the mall. They really *ought* to do something about their window displays."

"I've never seen you there. What's wrong with the windows?"

"*B-o-o-ring!* Always a season too late. Don't push ski outfits in January. Show swimwear. Get people in the mood for warm weather, worrying about how they'll look on the beach. Think of it — 'Sun on my Face,' '*Sur la Plage,'* 'Peach on the Beach,' 'Call of the Sea,' and all that. I mean, it's what clothing stores always do.''

''Well, we're not a trendy boutique. We sell serious equipment. Is that where you work, in a clothing store?''

He shook his head. ''You must know the Wax Works.''

Of course I did. It was the used record outlet of a big electronics store. On the other side of the mall from us. Everyone shopped there. ''I guess I never noticed you.''

He threw his head down and sang into the tablecloth. '' 'You can look right through me, walk right by me and never even know I'm there.' '' He lifted his head. ''I'm not surprised. I'm in charge of soundtracks and cast albums. I doubt you ever go in that department.''

He was right about that. I liked middle of the road stuff, none of that heavy metal or punk rock. Easy listening. Especially when I was in a romantic mood, like when Tony would fix us wine coolers, put on a record, and we'd relax with a couple of months' copies of *Runner's World.* Damn that Tony! Alec cleared the table and asked me if I'd rather hear *Saratoga* or *Tenderloin,* but I wasn't paying attention. I was thinking about Tony. I left Alec to his records and went to my room to brood in peace.

Tony was sure taking his sweet time about calling. He had to be missing me as much as I missed him. I wondered if I should go see him, dream up some excuse, like did I leave this or that at the house? But I'd vowed I wouldn't go crawling back. I could phone, that wouldn't be as bad as going over. Maybe if Alec went into his room and got lost in some song I could sneak into the living room and call. Suppose he wasn't there? We used to love Sunday nights, never left the house. Tony liked to watch *60 Minutes.* Said it made him a more aware person. He'd always end up getting mad at something on the show, and when Tony got mad he turned all red and that always turned me on. So we were usually hot at it before Andy Rooney ever got to the point. Who was Tony turning on tonight? Some rich bitch? Some hunk from his fancy gym? Or was he at the club prancing around in his Superman jock strap? How could he do this to me?

On top of all that, I was upset about what Alec had told me, about how people watched us and talked about us. I mean, sure, we knew people looked, especially gay guys. And we did stop in at the bar once in a while, just to, well, kind of let people know there were these two great-looking dudes who'd found each other. And I suppose we knew how we looked in those running shorts when the sweat was gleaming on our backs and chests. But I never really thought about people *talking* about us. How was I ever going to show up in a bar alone? I was done for. This was definitely not how things were supposed to be turning out. Damn that Tony. And damn that Alec for telling me! I never should have taken this room.

After another week I decided that peanut butter may have protein, but it gets pretty boring. Cooking for one is depressing, and there wasn't much I knew how to make anyway, so I started splitting the grocery bills with Alec. Why not, since he loved to cook? The kitchen looked like a hardware store, gadgets and machines everywhere; I had no idea what they were for. After I ran out of instant coffee I asked him if I could borrow a little, and he almost fainted.

''Instant coffee? In *my* kitchen?'' Then he taught me how to measure the beans and work the coffee mill and fold the filters. So what the hell, I'd be doing the guy a favor if I let him cook for me.

It didn't take long before we'd fallen into a routine. We were only together for dinner a few times a week; the other nights he left it warming for me. When he could stretch the leftovers, he even made lunch for me to take to work.

Otherwise I'd just grab something down at the mall. I never bothered much with breakfast — you can't run or work out on a full stomach. But Alec was always up bright and early, whipping up French toast or waffles or pancakes and telling me how important a good breakfast is. I resisted at first, but I'm only human, and the devil himself must have thought up French toast with real maple syrup. So I started changing my running time and going to the gym a little later and even began worrying about whether or not I'd fit into my spring wardrobe. What was the harm, I kept reminding myself, I was going to be out of the apartment before spring ever came.

SCENE III

Donnybrook

Those first few weeks Alec didn't go out much, either. He'd sing along with his records while he cleaned the place or wrote who knows what on his typewriter or cooked up special treats for dinner. As far as I could tell he didn't have any social life, and sometimes I wished he'd go out more. Not that I had any reason to be alone, but when it's just two of you there, night after night, you have no choice but to talk to each other and act friendly, and let's face it, Alec was not the kind of guy I had in mind for a friend.

As it turned out, I didn't know when I was well off. Once the new semester got under way at the university, all his friends came back to town and pretty soon our apartment was chirping and twittering with all sorts of little creatures. One was named Randy, a college kid, with light curly hair and a diamond in his ear, just the sweetest little thing, if you know what I'm saying. I mean, fem all the way. He always hung around with Tom, tall and skinny like Alec with a hawk nose and shiny black hair, and he *was,* I *must* say, just Miss *Melodrama,* with his arms waving, clutching at his throat and emphasizing every other word. I'd just started getting used to Alec when these two flamers showed up to bring out the worst in him. Of course he just had to introduce me to them, calling me his roommate, about which I had a few choice things to say later that night.

I thought of those two little flits as the Birdies, and they flew over two, three times a week, sometimes with other birds of a feather. I wouldn't have thought a small town like this could be home to so many flaming faggots, but I guess they migrated in for the school year. At least Alec got the message and stopped introducing me to all of them. They'd congregate in our living room and listen to Alec's records and have loud arguments about what they'd hear next. Tom would be just too depressed, so he needed something *really* up, but someone else would be going *crazy* because some tune had been running through his head and he just *had* to hear whatever. Most of the time I stayed in my room and tried not to listen to them, but once in a while I'd sort of get drawn into it with a curious fascination, like it was this whole other world they were getting worked up over. Especially when they fought about it. Were Adams and Strouse better than Bock and Harnick? Did Rodgers write better tunes with Hart than with Hammerstein? Or they'd dispute the relative merits of Gwen Verdon and Carol Channing, Jerry Orbach and Jack Cassidy, the "late great," as Alec always called him.

Worse yet, they'd have the same arguments over and over, trying to decide on the three or the five or the ten greatest scores, bickering over whether you could count anything before *Oklahòma!* because if not you'd have to leave out *Showboat,* but wasn't that really an operetta? And shouldn't Sondheim be in a class by himself, and hadn't *Candide* turned out to be an opera after all, and didn't *Camelot*'s music overwhelm the story, and could any of the numbers in the revival of *House of Flowers* measure up to the original? Finally they'd put on a record, which was always a relief, since I'd rather hear the music than their shouts: "Do you hear that?" "The man simply can't sing." "Did you catch that rhyme?" If I didn't listen too closely, I could swear I was down at the gym when the guys in the locker room started arguing over who was the best quarterback in the NFL or the three greatest pitchers to ever play the game or whether so-and-so would've KO'd what's-his-name if they'd gotten in the ring together. The Jocks and the Show Queens, I thought, maybe I should organize a bowling league.

When they weren't going on about the best and the worst, they'd play this game where one of them would pick a word and they'd have to name as many show songs as they could that had that word in it. Like once it was songs with "moon" in the title: "Moon in my Window," "The Man in the Moon," "Moon-faced, Starry-eyed," "What Good Would the Moon Be?," "Moonshine Lullaby," "Lazy Moon," "Musical Moon," "Devil Moon," "Desert Moon." And woe unto the jerk who didn't know which song came from *Goldilocks* and which from *Golden Rainbow.*

They called it a game, but more often than not they'd end up fighting. Like the time they were naming flowers: "Six Lillies of the Valley," "Heather on the Hill," "Edelweiss.". . .

"Crepe myrtle."

"That's not a title."

"We didn't say we were just using titles."

"Then gillyflowers. Something about a nice bowl of gillies."

"Instead of daisies."

"What?"

"That's what she says, gillyflowers instead of daisies. What the hell is a gillyflower, anyway?"

"How should I know? It's a flower, isn't it? You don't like it, then 'geraniums.' I should get double for that — the character who says it is named Daisy."

"Then I should get double for 'crepe myrtle' because it's from *House of Flowers.*"

"Doesn't count. You have to *name* a flower, not use the word 'flower,' that's a different game."

" 'Everything's Coming up Roses.' "

" 'I Won't Send Roses.' "

"I just used roses."

"Who said you can't repeat? Then daffodils. 'Everything's Coming Up Roses' mentions daffodils, too. Now I suppose you'll tell me I can't use the same song.

"We had gillyflowers and daisies from the same song."

"I took back the gillyflowers. Remember the geraniums?"

" 'Violets and Silverbells.' Two flowers, one song."

"No one ever said we were giving double scores. Magnolias."

"What's the line?"

"It's in *Mame*."

"He's right. Your turn."

"Which are you using, the violets or the silverbells?"

Is it any wonder I couldn't stand having these flakes around? This was enough to make a guy want to go out and stomp on a tulip. Alec, of course, knew more songs than any of them. He'd drive the rest of them crazy by telling them how many songs he could think of with the word coconut, or banana, or the name Delilah and make the others come up with them.

"There are at least six that mention Fred Astaire."

"Hints! Hints! It's not fair, you've had time to think them up. We need hints."

"OK, he was born in Omaha. His real name was Fred Austerlitz."

"We said hints, not a biography."

"Those are hints, it's all in the songs. Just ask Lila Tremaine. Think of cops dancing by. Or getting a new pair of shoes. Or tapping the other chaps to death. I'll make one easy, Astair-male rhymes with airmail."

Sometimes, when the feathers were flying, I'd feel like

a prisoner in my own room and wished they'd all get out. Then one night, the shit came mighty close to hitting the fan. They started out playing their game with London songs: "I'm in London Again," "London Is a Little Bit of All Right," "The Worst Pies in London," "King of London," "This Amazing London Town." They started arguing over whether they'd agreed that "London" had to be in the title or just mentioned in the song. That was when I tuned them out and turned on my radio — loud. So it came as something of a jolt when I thought I heard someone mention the name Tony. I turned the radio off and listened at the door. Sure enough, I heard "Tony" then heard it again. I wondered just what game they were playing now.

I was sure they were doing it to taunt me. Maybe because I'd had the radio up so loud. To tell the truth, I wasn't very nice to Alec's friends, didn't say hello, didn't act like I even noticed they were there. I mean, types like that, you don't want them to think you *approve* of them or anything. So this was how they were getting back at me, gossiping about Tony. I opened my door a crack; they'd put a record on, and I couldn't tell what they were carrying on over. But I did hear someone say Superman, so I figured they'd heard about his act and were discussing it to razz me. Well I'd show them. I put on my running shoes, changed into sweats, stomped out of the apartment and slammed the door so hard the needle jumped.

Later that night Alec told me he was sorry they'd been so loud. I said it wasn't so much how loud they were as who they were talking about that got to me, all that mention of Tony. At first Alec looked like he was going to burst out laughing. Lucky for him he didn't. He pulled himself together and looked down at the floor to try and keep his composure.

"I'm sorry, Joe. We were talking about the Tony awards, you know, like Oscars, but for the theater."

I was skeptical. ''Then what about Superman?''

''What about it? We were trying to remember if *It's a Bird, It's a Plane, It's Superman* had won any Tony awards. It's just a show.''

''It is? You mean like the movie?''

''Long before the movie — a Broadway musical. It's one of my favorites. Why?''

Needless to say, I felt like the shit had bounced off the fan and landed all over me. So they hadn't heard about Tony's act. After all, how could they? Tony never had anything to do with guys like them. At least Alec had the decency not to laugh at me. I shrugged off his question. ''Well, you guys really ought to keep it down, you know? I mean, if I'm going to live here I deserve some peace and quiet, don't I?''

''Sure,'' he said smiling. ''I'm really sorry. Look, I put away some cookies for you. Are you hungry?''

So we had some milk and cookies and listened to *Superman*. I even recognized a couple of the songs I'd heard Alec singing, including the line about the knish. And, I thought, if Tony had a little more imagination, he could've used some of the tunes in his routine. Poor Tony, he just wasn't a creative kind of guy.

SCENE IV

The Body Beautiful

Between the Birdies coming to call and Tony *not* calling, I thought I'd go nuts. The only thing that helped me keep my sanity those first few weeks was my exercise schedule. I'd been something of a track star in high school, forced into it, more or less, by the coach and my dad. My school was so small that any guy who could walk from point A to point B without falling down was expected to go out for a sport. Everyone said that with my size I'd be a natural for football, but I nixed that in my freshman year when a member of the team broke his nose and ended up looking like he'd been pressed between the pages of a book.

I wasn't about to risk spoiling my looks, so I agreed to join the cross-country team, since the worst you could do running was pull a muscle — not the kind of injury that shows or leaves scars. We'd take these long runs through the corn fields and pastures, slipping over the cow patties, pissing together in the bushes — a lot more fun than slamming your head into some two-hundred pound bozo.

I had the hots for the team captain, and I made myself keep up with him so we could talk and I could get a good look if he pulled off his shirt. Since he was the fastest guy on the team, I kind of accidentally became a winning runner. Running gets to be a habit, and I kept it up at the university. In the summer it lets me get an even tan without having to sit in one place, and in the winter it keeps my weight down. I was lucky that Tony was into running, too, since it's better with a buddy. He said it gave him the stamina he needed to stay on his feet all day. What I didn't know was that he already had more than enough stamina lying down.

It was hard getting used to running without Tony, but thanks to Alec's breakfasts and the Birdies' song fests, I was putting in more miles than ever, any time I got bored or restless or needed to get away from all the commotion. Whatever frustrations I didn't get rid of on the road I worked out at the gym. Helping my dad on the farm had always kept me in shape, and when I got to the university, I liked the fact that guys sometimes asked me if I worked out. So I signed up at the Nautilus to keep what I had — and to keep the guys looking. Besides, you only have to glance at catalogs and things to know that beefcake is in. Even the newspaper ads. Thank heaven for low-rise briefs!

Tony was eager to help me at the Nautilus, but even then he had his eye on the free weights in the back. Sure, he said, you could get strength and definition on the machines, but if you wanted to put on bulk, those weights were the only way to do it. But I like the machines; they're safe. You can't fall out or lose your balance or risk having something heavy drop on you, and an injury can undo months of hard work. There's something about those free weights that has me a little scared. I mean, those guys always look like they're about to rupture something, especially guys like Tony who are always showing off. Who knows, maybe if I'd gone along with him we'd still be together. But if I wasn't more to him than someone to work out with, the hell with him. I'll stick with my machines.

Anyway, sitting there, all strapped in, I can watch myself in the mirrors, see my muscles swell and my veins stand out and at the same time keep an eye on everyone else in the place. Once in a while, if you're lucky, some guy's balls'll pop out of his shorts on the hip and back machine, and the mirrors allow you to enjoy the view without letting on you're even looking.

Watching guys in the mirror may not sound like much, but you take what you can get. The Nautilus, unlike those big-city clubs, isn't cruisy, at least not that I know of. Besides, like I said, I'm always careful. The gym is full of gorgeous guys with fantastic bods, but one wrong move and a fellow could get hurt. Some of these men have macho down to an art — even bring their girlfriends along to change the weights for them. Guys like that I don't even look at in the mirror. Sure, I have a few pals there, to joke around with, but I have to listen to the ball scores and know the names of the coaches of the university teams; that's all these guys talk about, that and the women who work out. But it's just jock talk, and I try hard to fit in. Which isn't to say that some of those guys don't make it into my fantasies. But it's not like I get turned on in the shower room or anything. Something like that, a guy could *definitely* get hurt.

Now I had to change my workout schedule, not only because of those breakfasts Alec fixed, but also because I was tired of the regulars asking me where my buddy Tony was. People just expected us to be together. So I started going to the gym a little later than I used to, and pretty soon I noticed this one guy who seemed to watch those mirrors as much as I did. After our eyes met a few times he nodded, and I thought I might just be on to something here. It didn't take me long to find out his name was Jerry, and he had a body you wouldn't believe. Not stocky, like Tony, but with a slender, perfectly proportioned build and just the right amount of muscle. He told me he worked out six or seven days a week, with both machines and weights, and after I'd run into him a few times he asked if I'd spot him while he bench pressed. So I stood behind him like he told me to and looked down the length of those beautiful legs while his curly brown hair tickled the insides of my knees. Maybe there *was* something to be said for weight lifting after all.

When he was through he gave me a real nice smile and asked if he could spot me. I told him I wasn't into free weights, and he said he'd be glad to help me out if I decided to give them a try. My body, he said, had potential. So I started to time my visits to the club with his schedule and got it worked out to the point that we were ready to shower at the same time, just so I could check him out. Man, did he pass inspection! Of course, I had nothing to go on, really, except a couple of smiles in the mirror and my own imagination, so I knew I'd have to take it slow and not run any risks, just keep reading the sports pages in case he asked me if I'd heard who won over the weekend.

I was surprised at myself for even thinking about a new relationship, since I still expected to hear from Tony. But a month had passed and he hadn't gotten in touch, so I figured, what the hell, I'll make an effort and meet him half way. I dropped by the restaurant where he worked and stopped in at the bar. He'd have to see me when he filled his drink orders. I went on a Thursday, when I knew he had the lunch shift, and was on my third beer without even catching a glimpse of him.

I finally asked the bartender. He told me Tony'd quit the week before. My stomach dropped about three stories when I heard that. "After the feast, the fast," grandma always used to say. February is not a good month to start a diet.

SCENE V

Follies

The Birdies came over one night feeling depressed about the cold, snowy weather. They were trying to cheer themselves up by thinking of "good times" songs. They'd been through "Good Times Are Here To Stay," "Hello, Good Times," "The Best of Times," "This Time It's the Big Time," and were arguing about whether or not "It's High Time" fit the theme. I, for one, was not having a high time and was hidden away in my room, as usual, studying my feet. I may look tough, but the fact is, I bruise easily. I mean, I sweep out the kitchen and when I'm finished there's a blister on my finger; I bump into a chair and I'm black and blue. So running is a problem because I keep getting these ugly purple toenails. They come from running on hills, and around here there's no avoiding hills. Good for the calves, hell on the toes. Takes months for them to grow out. Once in a while it pays off in the locker room at the gym, because I can put my foot on a bench, give my toes a clinical once-over, and pretty soon some guy might notice and say "gross" and the next minute we're talking and comparing injuries. Next to ball scores, guys love to talk about where it hurts. Even better, they like to show you.

Anyway, that particular night I'd been trimming the last bit off a toenail that had finally grown out, and it looked good as new. The Birdies had gotten tired of their musical game and started twittering about some play the university was going to put on that spring. I'd given up trying not to listen to them. Whenever I managed to tune them out, I'd end up thinking about Tony, and anything was better than that. So I gave my toes a final inspection while they carried on about the upcoming auditions. Tom and Randy both planned to try out, and they were bitching that there weren't enough good male roles. Randy said if he didn't get the part of the husband there was absolutely *no way* he was going to take the diamond out of his ear, and Tom just *knew* he was too tall for the drag role. When I heard that, I knew this play wasn't up my alley. Alec said that at least *Chicago* was relatively recent and innovative and a lot better than having to suffer through yet another production of *Sweet Charity* or *The Fantasticks.* Then they started to gossip about the director, who was new that year, and whether or not he was gay. Tom swore the guy had patted his behind at least twice at the first sign-up, and Randy said Tom's imagination was in his ass and that Tom could stand in line at the dry cleaner and insist someone had patted his behind, and if he kept feeling things maybe he'd better give himself a good dousing with A-200. And besides, Randy said, who cares whose behind gets patted, he wasn't going to sleep *his* way to a better part and if Tom did, he'd kill him. Since Alec knew more about those shows than anyone, I wondered why he wasn't trying out, too. He could sing and act and imitate just about anybody, and he really deserved a bigger audience than me. I supposed only university students were eligible.

Alec had put an end to the loud cat parties, and I guess I'd gotten used to having the Birdies around, like background noise. Of course I talked to them when I had to, when I answered the phone or opened the door. One at a time, they weren't as bad as they were together, and when they were together, I had to admit their campy humor could be pretty funny. I just didn't want them to know I thought so. After a while we observed what might best be called an uneasy truce. I suppose that night I was paying more attention than usual to what they were saying in order to keep my mind off my toes — I'd nicked myself with the nail clipper, and the sight of my own blood sometimes makes me a little nauseous. Once the bleeding stopped, I gave up on their chit-chat and was about to have a look at my checkbook to see if I could afford a couple of pairs of aviator sunglasses I'd seen in a catalog; they came in six colors, and I'd have a hard time making a choice. My concentration was broken all of a sudden when I heard another voice, which sounded familiar but which took me a minute or two to place. Then I realized they must've turned on the TV to hear Harold Waldman give one of his movie reviews on the local station.

Now if there was one voice I *really* couldn't stand, it was Harold Waldman's. Harold was this flaming fiftyish faggot who somehow managed to turn himself into a local celebrity, mainly because his reviews were more like comedy routines than anything else. He joked about himself a lot, and that seemed to make it OK for him to act like a fool. Most people thought he was a scream. He embarrassed me. Like the time he came on with his hair permed into ringlets. "It's the Annie look, gang," he shrieked. "If it makes the kid cute it must make me absolutely adorable." Or the time he pouted at the cameraman, "Couldn't we smear some vaseline on the lens? I had a bad night." Everywhere you went, people would ask, "Did you catch Harold last night?" and crack up. They'd never seen him done up in full drag on Halloween or drunk under a table, running his hands up all the legs he could reach. I, of course, hadn't either, since Harold and I hardly traveled in the same circles, but Tony had told me all about it. Tony knew a lot, for someone who never went out much.

One thing was clear, Harold didn't know diddly-shit

about movies. ''Make up your own minds, kiddies,'' he'd tell his viewers, ''don't listen to me.'' Profound. Except it was hard not to listen to him. He was on three nights a week, at 6:30 and 11.

I stuck my head out the bedroom door and was about to yell to Alec to turn down the TV when what do I see but idiot Harold *right there* in the apartment, having a hissy fit because the library threatened to cut off his card if he didn't bring back his books. ''How am I going to prepare my Bette Davis festival,'' he screamed, ''if I have to return the books? Do they think I just make this stuff up?'' He glanced at me before I could duck back into my room and clutched his chest with both hands. Talk about limp-wristed faggots, with all the heart pounding and chest grabbing these guys did, they must have had wrists of iron. Harold's mouth fell open for an instant of welcome silence, then, without taking his eyes off me, he started in again. ''What *do* we have here? Alec, you didn't tell me you were running a sweet shop in the spare bedroom.''

''That's just my roomma. . . . He shares the apartment. Don't pay any attention to him.''

''Don't pay attention? I'm dazzled. *Blinded!* Come here and let me worship at the shrine of your physique.''

Unfortunately I did look awfully good just then. I was still barefoot, and my jeans were undone so I could reach my toes better, and I was wearing a new sleeveless T-shirt I'd been trying on to see how my biceps looked. I was planning to introduce it into my workout wardrobe, but only if my upper arms were prominent enough to do it justice. Pink wasn't usually my color, but a lot of guys wear purple or lavender at the gym. Jerry, I'd noticed, favored turquoise.

''Joe,'' Alec said, ''this is Harold Waldman. You probably recognize him. That's Joe.''

''Well, 'happiness is just a thing called Joe.' Come over here, you thing.''

"Alec, I'm kind of busy. Do you think you guys could keep it down in here?"

"Keep it down?" Harold gurgled. "While you're standing there with your muscles hanging out?"

I retreated to my room and turned on the radio. I was thinking I'd really have to get out of that place and away from those Nellie queens. Time to start looking for a new apartment. As soon as it stopped snowing.

It turned out Harold and Alec were good friends. If you can call people who fight all the time friends. A couple of weeks after I'd first met Harold, I came home in a really good mood. Jerry had wanted to do curls over the top edge of the slant board and asked me to spot him; I had to lay my arm on the board and grab his wrists. I was careful not to hold on too long or too tight, but I sure liked it. In the locker room he thanked me and told me again I ought to do free weights because I had a good build and could really put on muscle. So I began to think maybe he was right. He always smiled at me when our eyes met in the mirror, but as long as I was strapped into those machines and he was over on the weight mats, this relationship was getting nowhere. So when he asked me to spot him it was always a high point of my day.

But good moods don't last when you get to the landing and hear Alec and Harold yelling at each other. If I hadn't had to change for work, I wouldn't even have gone in.

"Harold," Alec was shouting, "what do shopping carts have to do with movie reviews?"

"I told you, I was talking about my pet peeves. Dirty theaters, slobs who talk during the movie. Well, I don't like it when people leave shopping carts all over the parking lot. It detracts from the film-going experience."

"Since when did going to the movies become a full-fledged *experience*? I don't know what a minute of TV time costs, Harold, but I don't think the station expects their movie reviewer to waste it griping about shopping carts."

"Just wait and see my mail. I'll bet people loved it."

"People love roasted marshmallows. But you don't see them devoting air time to marshmallows. Shopping carts are irrelevant! They are *not* entertainment. Joe, tell Harold if shopping carts are entertaining."

"Harold makes everything entertaining. Harold *is* entertainment." I could tell by his look that Alec caught my meaning, but Harold beamed.

"There, you see?" Harold interrupted, before Alec could say anything. "My public knows what to expect from me."

"That's the problem," Alec yelled. "You've developed this *persona*. . . ."

"Don't start using that technical crap on me," Harold shouted back. "I have my fans and they don't know from personas."

They were still going at it when I shut my door and tried to remember the feel of Jerry's wrists in my hands. Then I studied myself in the mirror and tried to picture how I'd look with definition *plus* muscle. Was Jerry worth the risk of free weights?

SCENE VI

Celebration

"Harold's not too bright, is he?" I asked Alec that night.

" 'Lord knows he ain't got the smarts,' " he sang back at me.

"Then why do you put up with him?"

He shrugged and said he'd grown accustomed to his face. "The truth is, he needs me." I watched him. Sometimes I could just tell that the old record changer in his head was switched on. Sure enough, he began "As Long as He Needs Me." Then he turned to me. "Really, Harold is very insecure, doesn't do anything without asking me what I think." Then it was time for "He Needs Me Now," after which he said, "It's true. I give him his best ideas."

I was more than a little skeptical about that — I mean, Harold was an asshole, but he was a well-known asshole. Even the guys down at the store didn't go see a film if Harold hadn't liked it. And he did teach at the university. And who, after all, was Alec?

But I let it drop; there was no point arguing with him, not over something as trivial as Harold. Besides, he'd already launched himself into a medley of songs with the word "need" and I didn't want to interrupt his rendition of Streisand and people needing people. The fact was, except for those friends of his, we were getting along pretty well. He could act fairly normal when he wanted, if you can call singing songs instead of making conversation normal. I wasn't even sure when he was saying his own words and when he was doing lyrics, so I figured whenever he didn't quite make sense, it must've been a line from a song. At least I hoped so. If not, he was one weird dude. But he was, I had to admit, a great cook.

One night when I got home from the store, the apartment smelled especially good. "What's for dinner?" I asked, immediately regretting the question. It sounded a little too domestic.

"Something special," was all he would say. It sure was special. For the first course he set some kind of flaky pastry in front of me. "Baked brie," he announced, *"en croûte."*

Now this stuff wasn't the kind of food you eat when your'e contemplating free weights. What you need is beef. Red meat. But one taste of that cheese and I wasn't going to complain. Besides, after that he served a terrific stew, even though he called it *daube à la Provençale.* And for dessert, a chocolate mousse.

"What's the occasion, Alec?"

"I thought you'd *never* ask. As of today you've been here six weeks."

"What's the big deal about that?"

"Oh, nothing. A minor victory for me, one small step for Show Queens. I haven't scared you away."

"Yeah, well, it's been so cold I haven't felt like looking for a new place. And I've, you know, given this number to people."

"Whatever," he said, smiling as he dished up seconds on dessert. "You think maybe you'd like to do something tonight? A movie?"

"With you?"

He rolled his eyes. "Yes, with me. Would I ask if I expected you to go alone? I mean, I wouldn't want to be accused of prying into your hectic social life, but neither of us goes out much. I just thought I'd ask."

It was true. Except for an occasional night out with Harold, he rarely went anywhere. Though he more than made up for it by having the Birdies over or twittering away on the phone with them. I wondered what he did for sex, assuming he did anything. I figured he must have something going with one of the Birdies. Surely not with Harold; *he* wouldn't be able to shut up long enough.

"So?"

"So? What?"

"So, 'a needle pulling thread.' The movie! Do you want to go? Look in the paper and pick whatever you like."

"You're not getting any ideas, are you?"

"What kind of ideas?"

"About us?"

"For Christ's sake! I asked you if you wanted to go to a movie. I don't plan to sit in the back row and hold hands. Forget it."

I guess I shouldn't have said it, but this whole thing about celebrating my still being here, the fancy dinner and all. . . . Still, he *had* gone to a lot of trouble. "I'll go if you want. I didn't mean to insult you."

"I'll be totally butch. Sneak cigarettes, roll beer bottles under the seats, make farting noises during the love scenes — no one will suspect a thing."

So we went to a Clint Eastwood picture. I don't think it's what Alec would have chosen, and to tell the truth, it wasn't really my first choice, either. But I felt I had an image to keep up, and I didn't want him to think we had too much in common or that I planned to make this a habit. We didn't see anyone we knew, and when we got back to the apartment, he offered me a brandy.

"Did I pass? Can you be seen in public with me?"

"Aw, Alec. You're OK. I mean, when you want to be.

But when those friends of yours are here. . . .You flame as much as they do.''

''It's just harmless fun.'' He started to shimmy as he sang a few bars of ''All in Fun.'' ''I suppose you don't like it when I do that, either.''

''What, sing? It's odd, but I guess I'm used to it. Aren't you ever serious about anything?''

''It's better not to get too serious.''

''Why's that?''

''No point in bringing up unpleasant things.''

''Who says being serious means being unpleasant?''

''Let's not get into this. Let's be happy. That's it! 'Happy Talk,' 'Sing Happy,' 'Walking Happy,' 'The Happy Time,' 'I Want to Be Happy,' 'The Most Ha . . . .' ''

''Knock it off, Alec. Save the games for your friends. What is it, anyway? Don't you think I'm smart enough for you to talk seriously to me?''

''I have nothing serious to say.''

''I guess you don't like me much, do you?''

''Am I supposed to?''

''We're *supposed* to be roommates. I mean apartment mates. Not friends. Maybe I say some things I shouldn't. I'll try to be nicer to you.''

''And to my friends?''

''Alec, I just don't like people like them. They're stereotypes. It gives us all a bad name.''

'' 'Oh, you pompous, pompous, pompous, pompous ass!' There, I'm quoting songs again, so we can end this conversation now.''

''Alec, the dinner was very nice. Going out to the movie was OK, and thanks for the brandy. I think we can get along if you just don't expect me to like your friends. All right?''

''If you say so.'' He refilled our glasses. ''Have you heard from your pal Tony?''

"I don't want to talk about him."

"Now who doesn't want to be serious?"

"No, I haven't heard from him. Why?"

He shrugged. "Nothing. Something I heard, that's all."

"What have you heard?"

"Just that he's working in the city. In some sort of club."

"You mean that he's a stripper? I know all about that. Who told you?"

"No one in particular. I just heard."

"Alec, *who* told you?"

"For cryin' out loud. Everybody's talking about it. It's not like it's a secret. I thought that's why you two broke up, anyway."

"And who told you *that?* Or is that general knowledge on the fag grapevine, too?"

"Well, I told you before everyone knew about the two of you. I'm sorry I brought it up."

"Yeah, well, it's over, so it's no big deal. I'm going to bed."

It was over, all right, there was no denying that. And there was no denying that life at the moment wasn't offering much. The apartment, the gym, the store, day after day. I remembered what grandma used to tell me. "There's no shame in falling, only in lying down too long." It was time I picked myself up and got my life back on track. OK, so that guy Jerry smiled at me in the mirror. I had to find out what was on his mind besides showing off his perfect teeth. If I didn't get hustling, life was going to be baked brie and brandy with Alec.

SCENE VII

Gentlemen Prefer Blondes

You'd probably think that a hot-looking guy who was known all over town as half of a perfect hunk couple would know plenty of gay men. But not counting Alec and his flock, I didn't know any, and I wasn't about to ask *them* to introduce me around. Seems like my problems always went right back to Tony.

Tony was, well, not exactly a snob — the word he liked to use was "exclusive." "We gotta be exclusive," he always told me, till it became a kind of buzzword. We couldn't shop in a certain store because it wasn't exclusive, or talk to certain people, or even wear certain clothes, because they weren't exclusive. We were special, he said, people noticed us, even envied us, and we had to act the way exclusive people act. That's why we wore those sexy running shorts and only stopped at the bar once in a while for a quick drink. I shouldn't have been surprised that people talked about us, we set ourselves up for it, but I guess I never stopped to think what it was they might be saying. And all this talk about being exclusive never prepared me for Tony running off to shake his buns in a strip joint. I should've asked him about that.

So it was going to be hard for me to get into circulation, especially now that everyone knew what my recently departed ex was up to in the city. Even before I met Tony,

I never really made the gay scene. I don't like to talk about that part of my life because, well, it wasn't really exclusive. Tony liked to tell me he was saving me from my own worst instincts. I believed him. Given some of his instincts, he should talk.

See, I met Tony in a tea room on campus. I know, a tea room, tacky tacky, but it wasn't really like that. I mean, it was a *campus* tea room at a reputable university, not some public shopping center or bus station john. Now I've known for a long time what my sexual preference is, ever since I was a little kid roughhousing under the sheets with my brother. He invented this game he called Squirrel, the point being to grab the other guy's nuts when he wasn't expecting it. My brother was older than me and bigger than me, and he only dreamed up games he knew he could win. But this game, which he'd come up with as just another way to get the better of me, this was one he always lost. So of course, he put a quick end to it. Then, when I was about ten, I had this friend Chuck, and we'd play blind man. One of us would close his eyes and pretend he was blind and the other would have to lead him around by the hand, tell him when to step up or down or turn. Well, when Chuck noticed that we'd always end up in the bushes behind the garage, he wouldn't be the blind man anymore. And I couldn't be, because his hand on my arm always gave me a hard-on. So I *knew.* But it was a small town in the middle of a cornfield, and a boy who carried his books the wrong way didn't make it off the school bus with his pants on, and a guy who glanced at another guy's dick in the shower after gym class had all the snapping towels aimed at his ass. So you get used to hiding, playing things close to your chest. And to staying clear of fems and swishes and even people like Alec who might be just a little. . .weird. They didn't play show tunes down at the grange hall.

I'd already suspected that gay men sometimes met

each other in toilets. When I was in high school, the guys would sometimes drive the forty miles to the county seat, where no one knew them, to guzzle beer. I went along in order to fit in, and because I liked being out with other boys. Friday nights were the best — that's when all the girls were busy learning flower arranging at the 4-H. Anyhow, we'd stop at this rest area along the interstate on our way home, to puke or, at the very least, take a good long leak, and we'd laugh at the things written on the walls. I didn't really believe that stuff, which is to say I didn't know what to believe; I figured there was one pervert who wrote it all himself in different handwriting. And I sure wasn't about to sneak back to find out. That's not something you risk when your dad plays pinochle with the county sheriff every Wednesday night, and everybody knows what kind of car everybody else drives. But I thought about that john a lot, and when I got to the university, it didn't take me long to follow the graffiti to the tea room down a flight of stairs in the basement of the union. When I found that tea room, I reckoned I'd found a home.

It wasn't that simple. Oh, I didn't need more than a few visits to figure out the mechanics, the signals and notes and stuff, but what did take a while was discovering that most of the guys who went down there weren't looking for what I was looking for — a boyfriend. In the beginning, I thought I had it made, that every gay guy on campus must go into that place, and that at least some of them would jump at the chance to settle down with someone like me. A lot of them, it turned out, were just in it for themselves. They'd get their rocks off first, and if I was still ready and willing, they had no second thoughts about making a getaway before I was able. Once in a while a guy might invite me back to his place and we'd have a hot time — hugging and kissing and all the good stuff. But it would always end with "see ya around," and if I did see him around, he'd act like I was a total stranger. I was confused and a little bit hurt, and finally I learned not to expect too much. The tea room was OK, up to a point. But I wanted a man to call my own. A real man.

In the meantime, if I had to settle for what I could get, I'd at least get it on my own terms, without being cheap and promiscuous in that john. I slipped in and out real fast and covered the peep hole with toilet paper until I was good and ready to have a look. And I'd always check the other guy out carefully — you wouldn't catch me being fooled by some old man who thinks he's pulling a fast one by wearing running shoes and Levis. I'd hang way down under the partition and get a good view. And if I couldn't see him without giving away too much of me, I had this other little trick. I'd put my books and my coat down next to my foot, and while the other guy was staring at the floor trying to get a fix on my shoe, I'd jump up onto the toilet and look down over the top of the partition, give him a good once-over while he'd be searching for a tapping toe. Scared a few guys right out of their hard-ons — and their stall.

But if someone measured up, I didn't mess around. None of this endless note writing, this "describe yourself" and "what do you like?" shit scribbled out on toilet paper. Either the guy was ready for action or he wasn't, and if he wasn't, the paper went right back into the peep hole and I was gone. No one was going to beat me out to wait around at the top of the stairs or catch sight of me in the mirror. No way. This was my game. I only made it with maybe half the guys I ran into down there. I guess even then I was exclusive, in my own way.

Of course other guys tried hard to get a look at me, and I guess some of them managed a quick glimpse because after a while I started noticing a theme in the graffiti on the walls — references to the "blond mystery man" or the "blond beauty." I knew they meant me because they'd mention times I'd been down there, after a certain class on a certain day. Sometimes I even wrote my own graffiti, which I'd sign "the blond phantom." But I did become more careful about varying the times of my visits. Sure, it was nice to be a tea room legend, but it was making it increasingly hard to keep from being identified. So I was lucky when Tony came along.

I think about that day a lot. There was no one down there when I arrived, so I was catching up on the latest scribblings on the walls. I'd just found this note, "to the blond beauty I met Thurs. at 2:45, how about a rerun? Make date." I was trying to remember who it was I'd met that day at 2:45, when Tony came down the stairs, except of course, I didn't know yet it was Tony. The most exciting part of the tea room is the beginning, some guy getting settled in the next stall, putting down his books, taking off his coat, opening his belt. You take advantage of his activity to check out his shoes, his pants, try to get a fix on his age. My first glimpse of Tony's hairy calf really turned me on, and the more I saw, the better it looked. And talk about not wasting time, he must have been hard before his ass even hit the seat.

Normally I made it a rule to keep things to a minimum, not do anything that would give my identity away, just the basics: looking, touching, under the wall sucking. But pretty soon we were doing things under that partition you wouldn't have thought two guys could do. Finally I threw caution to the wind and slid under to his side with my stall door still locked, the blond phantom revealed. When he suggested, a good forty-five minutes later, that we go upstairs for coffee, I had nothing to lose, and that was the last time I've been in the tea room. And why I couldn't go back. People had seen me around with Tony. If I went anywhere near that john I'd be recognized, the mystery man a mystery no more. And besides, what's a peep hole after a year with Tony?

If the men's room was out, the only other place I knew to meet people was the bar, this place near campus where guys hang out, late, after 11. There was this unspoken rule that somewhere around 10:30 the college kids and locals moved out and the gays came in. Once in a while, Tony told me, a new bar would open up downtown, and the gays would drift down to check it out. But it would be too far from campus or the townies would hassle them, so they'd head back to this first place, the Alamo. That's where Tony and I stopped in, once or twice a month, just to let people know we were going strong. The prospect of walking in alone now was kind of scary, so I was getting awfully well acquainted with my left hand. And more and more I kept thinking about this guy Jerry at the gym. He *was* friendly, and he did wear turquoise shirts, once with purple pants. So maybe I'd start doing free weights and he'd be my new workout buddy. Couldn't hurt to try.

The next time I saw him, after I'd spotted him on his bench presses I said I'd like to do a little lifting myself. He was very encouraging, showed me all the basic stuff, squats, flies, and so on. Better yet, he showed me what each routine would do, outlining my muscles with his finger. ''Feel this,'' he'd say, nodding at his shoulder or arm when he lifted. The good part was that we seemed to spend half the time that day feeling each other. The bad part was that afterward I hurt like hell.

Grin and bear it, I told myself. Remember, no pain, no gain.

SCENE VIII

How to Succeed in Business

If my social life consisted of nothing but me, my mirror, and feeling Jerry's muscles, things weren't going much better down at the store. I'd started working as soon as I hit town; I had to. Times were hard for farmers, and my folks weren't all that keen on my going off to school in the first place. If I wanted an education, they said, I could fit in some night-school classes at the local junior college — after the chores were done. But I wanted to be where the action was. Not to mention the men.

I didn't mind working. I felt like a real city boy, with a job to go to and money in my pocket. The place where I worked sold hard-core athletic stuff, serious equipment, top of the line. We didn't go in for frills or fancy displays. And the guys who worked there, we all knew our stuff. I mean, we were into fitness. We *did* it, we didn't just talk about it. A select bunch of guys.

The problem was, we hadn't had a very good Christmas that winter, at least not like we'd hoped, and the January sales hadn't moved enough inventory. There were rumors that someone might even be laid off. So we were pretty glum when Bud, the store manager, called a meeting of the whole staff one night after we'd closed. Bud was an OK guy, a real hunk, wrestler-type build, but easygoing. We knew a meeting like this meant something big was up.

"All right, guys," he said, "here's the bottom line. We've got the location, we've got the merchandise, we've got the demographics. We've also got the lowest sales volume per square foot of any athletic store in town. What I want to know is, what are we going to do about it?" The eight of us squirmed and looked at each other. Bud stood there, tapping his foot. "Ideas, guys, we need ideas. My ass is on the line here along with all of yours, so let's get thinking. Ralph?"

"Yes sir?" I could tell he was nervous; no one ever called Bud "sir."

"Ideas, Ralph. What can we do to turn this place around?"

"Uh, let's see, sir. Maybe we could try to be friendlier. You know, make sure we say 'have a nice day' to everyone."

Bud put his hand on his forehead and mumbled "Say 'have a nice day.' " Then he sighed. Ralph was sweating. Bud looked around. "Well, it's a start. Jimmy? Any ideas?"

"No sir, but I'll sure work on it."

Bud looked at each of us, one after the other. I felt like his eyes were burning a hole in me. "Joe?" I looked into my lap and said a few words. "Speak up, Joe. If you've got something to say, let's hear it."

"The windows," I repeated, louder this time. "We ought to do something about the windows."

"What about the windows?"

"'Well, they're boring. I know we've never gone in for trendy displays and all, but really, winter's almost over and we're still pushing ski clothes. No one wants to be reminded it's winter. We should be featuring swimwear." A couple of the guys snickered, but I figured, what the hell, it's every man for himself. "Have you looked over in Goldsmith's department store? It's all spring fashions. And Cordone Bros., menswear, all warm weather stuff. That's what stores *do,* you know, get people to look forward to what's coming up. We should be making everybody think about getting in shape for summer."

Ralph and Jimmy looked at each other like to say I was nuts, and I heard someone mutter something about fruit-cakes being for Christmas. I just kept my eyes on Bud, who was rubbing his chin.

"Joe, you're right. We've neglected our windows. Best advertising we've got, and it's free. Talk to me tomorrow, Joe, tell me what's on your mind." He lightened up. "Now we're on the right track. OK, you guys, anything else?"

A couple of them managed to come up with a few suggestions — widening the aisles, running a contest, offering student discounts. I was hoping Bud would let us go, tell us to sleep on it, but he wasn't letting up. Finally his gaze fell on me again. I felt like I was back in school and the teacher needed to know *someone* had read the assignment. Now one thing I'd noticed when I started going to the gym a little later in the day was how many women were in the place. Sometimes it was all I could do to find another guy to stare at in the mirrors. It was like being in a damn sorority house. You'd lie down on the leg curl machine and find yourself in a cloud of perfume. And if you dared sweat, some dainty little thing would throw you a dirty look and wipe off the cushion with a towel. Or a two-year-old might stare you down while you were doing back extensions on the Roman chair because his mother was off in the tanning room. So when Bud kept looking at me like that, counting on me, I decided to go for it.

"I was thinking," I began, "down at the gym, the Nautilus, a lot of women work out. Maybe we should try to appeal more to women."

The other guys were smirking and making wisecracks. Jimmy whispered something about bringing in potted petunias. Bud frowned at him, then turned back to me. "Appeal to women how?"

I squirmed and swallowed and finally said it. "Well, at the gym, when a woman signs up, they ask her if she wants a female instructor, you know, to make her feel more at ease. Maybe we should hire a woman." Bud looked at everyone again, not saying anything, just thinking.

"That's all we need," Jimmy grumbled, "some chick tying up the staff john. I suppose we'll have to start closing the door to a take a leak."

Ralph grinned. "Yeah, but if it was the *right* woman. . . ."

Bud cut them short. "I want you all to keep thinking about this for a few days. At least Joe here is on the ball."

I left not knowing what he really thought about my ideas, but I'd managed to come through in the crunch. I didn't even care when Jimmy called me a brown nose and asked me if I'd decided on the color of the petunias. That was the kind of comment that normally would have made me nervous about having blown my cover, but this time I had other things on my mind, like what I'd tell Bud when he asked me about the windows. I figured Alec would help me if I ran into trouble, and in the meantime, dreaming up displays might be fun, something to occupy me when I needed to hide in my room so I wouldn't have to listen to arguments about the ten best this or that.

Within a week, Jimmy was fired and a girl hired in his place. Judy was a phys. ed. major up at the university, and her goal in life was to be a girls' volleyball coach. She was the kind of gal that we used to call "healthy" back home. Ralph said she had the build of a station wagon. He was especially pissed because he'd had such high hopes. "A girl her size had to pick volleyball," he said. "Less ground to cover." The other guys weren't much better. They seemed to blame me for her being hired, like it was my fault Bud hadn't picked some big-boobed blond. Just my luck, he tapped me to show her the ropes.

Now Ralph was hardly the brightest guy in the world, but he sure had a mouth on him, and after a few days I overheard him telling the other guys that Judy had all the earmarks of a lez. Pretty soon they were all convinced of it. And the better I knew her, the more I was sure they were right.

Now I've got nothing against gay women. On the contrary. In an ideal world, the ratio of straight to gay men would be reversed, and I wouldn't want to see all the women left high and dry — I mean, the less competition, the better. So if there are women who like to make it with other women, and can figure out how to go about it, more power to them. But that doesn't mean they shouldn't act like women. And as sure as there are fems and flits on the male side, there are some butch lesbians who cross the line, too. Now I'm not saying Judy was an out-and-out dyke, but she was obvious enough that an idiot like Ralph could spot her, and that had me worried. The last thing I needed was for her to figure *me* out, to treat me like the two of us had some little secret in common. So I did what I had to do to show her around the store, but at the same time, I tried to keep my distance. Unfortunately, Judy came on like gangbusters.

"Going to stuff the crotch?" she asked me while I was adjusting a tank suit on a male dummy.

"I'll leave the fun part to you," I told her. "I'm only doing this because Bud told me to." Actually, Bud hadn't told me anything like that. After I'd made some suggestions for brightening up the windows, he put me in charge of the displays and said to do whatever I wanted. So I was turning the window into a beach scene, a big yellow sun, paper umbrellas. After a couple of people all bundled up in their coats and scarves stopped to look at the swimsuits, Bud started getting into it himself, even talked about ordering a load of sand to dump in the display. Then he asked me if I had any other ideas to liven up the store. I suggested, for starters, that we tack sweat socks onto the wall in a big flower pattern, to show how many colors they came in. I'll be damned if he didn't tell me to go ahead and do it. I half-expected someone to make another crack about potted petunias, but after what happened to Jimmy, nobody dared say a word. Except Judy.

"You've got hidden talents, Joe," she said, looking up at me when I was on the top rung of a ladder and couldn't escape. "I figured you must be smarter than you look."

It seemed every time I turned around, there she was. She'd somehow heard about the meeting we'd had with Bud and had gotten it into her head, no doubt from something Ralph said, that I was responsible for her getting the job.

"I'm really grateful," she kept telling me. "This job means a lot to me."

"I had nothing to do with it. Bud does the hiring."

"I know, I know, but you made it possible. You're an OK guy, not like these other dumbos. You're different. I think we can be friends."

This was just the direction I didn't want us headed in. "What do you mean, different?"

"The other guys haven't been able to accept me. Not that I care what they think. But you, you at least talk to me."

"Bud told me to help you out. I only talk to you because you bug me all the time about how I got you hired, which I didn't."

"You can deny it all you want, Joe, but I know better. Feminine intuition. We're a lot alike, you and I. Besides, everyone needs a friend."

"Judy, I got all the friends I can handle." Which was about as big a lie as I've ever told.

SCENE IX

Good News

Judy may have been giving me a hard time, but Bud gave me a raise. And a lot of praise for what I'd done for the store. I hadn't mentioned any of this yet to Alec, since pulling tank suits onto naked dummies wasn't something to brag about, and besides, I was a little embarrassed at having stolen his idea and passing it off as my own. But a raise *was* something to be proud of, so I was anxious to get home that night and tell him the good news. Which is why I wasn't too happy when I got to the top of the stairs and heard Harold's voice shrieking inside the apartment. He and Alec were in the middle of another big argument, and I don't think they even saw me come in. Tom and Randy were there, too, flitting around, trying to quiet the other two. I snuck into my room and tried to distract myself by thinking up ways to display jump ropes, but they were going at it so loud I couldn't concentrate. At first I figured it must have been some dumb thing, like all their arguments, who could sing better than who or what the rules were for whatever version of their games they were playing. But instead of it ending with Alec putting on a record, I heard the door slam and the Birdies trying to calm him down. Finally he told them to leave, too, and the door slammed again. So I waited a few minutes and peeked into the living room. Alec was sitting on the sofa staring at the ceiling.

"Alec? You OK?"

"I'm fine, now that Harold is gone."

"Maybe for good?"

He heaved a sigh. "Of course not. Tomorrow he'll call to apologize and tell me I was right. He knows I'm always right. Tell me what you think about this. . . ."

"I'd just as soon stay out of it. This movie and musical stuff isn't my bag."

"That's why you'll be a good judge. Harold gives a film class every year, right? Picks out a dozen films that are supposed to illustrate some theme. So what is he proposing for next fall?" He looked at me like I was supposed to answer.

"What?"

"Films that lost the Academy Award. Did you ever hear of anything so stupid? I mean, what kind of theme is that? Films that lost! And those kids will get four credits?"

"Yeah, I've heard about his classes." Harold's course was famous on campus, a real gut, Mickey Mouseville. You watch these films every week, listen to Harold's "lecture" about the star's private life, then write an "emotion paper" where you tell how the film made you feel. You could write anything, this film made me feel good, this film made me feel bad. If you filled the page and got it in on time, you had an A. There was this story going around a few years ago about how after one picture Harold asked some kid how he felt. This clown'd been sitting in the back of the auditorium swilling beer like all the fraternity guys do in Harold's class, so the kid says, "I feel like I wanna barf." And Harold says, "I'll accept that." From then on everyone started calling the papers barf papers, and Harold's course was known as barf films, or someone might tell you he was taking barf's class. Finally, so they say, somebody scribbled "Waldman is barf" on a john wall right in Harold's own department, which, the story goes, Harold himself changed to "*Professor* Waldman is barf." So an argument like the one Alec just had with him hardly seemed important, since it didn't matter what films Harold showed.

"Alec, how on earth did he ever get hired up there, anyway?"

"God only knows. Harold's one of those people who looks good on paper. He's like a slow poison — if you don't get sick after the first exposure, you build up a tolerance."

"Well, he's not worth getting worked up over. Why do you care? Why put up with him?"

He shrugged. "He's good for laughs. And he's a good person to know. He gets freebies to everything. I've seen some great stuff, thanks to him, big shows in the city, musicals on their pre-Broadway tryouts. And like I told you, he needs me to help him with his reviews, just like he needs me to tell him when his course ideas suck. And you've got to admit, he's probably the most famous guy in town."

"How'd you ever manage to get mixed up with him?"

"It just happened. He was sort of courting me, inviting me places, asking my opinions. I was young and he was a professor. . . I suppose I was flattered. At least till I realized how dumb he was. Then I felt sorry for him."

"Doesn't it bug you? Him getting all the glory for your ideas?" I still wasn't sure how much of this was true, but the more I saw of Harold, the more I believed Alec.

"I don't like being in the spotlight. I get too nervous. Harold's all right. At least he can be. I guess I like him." He got a goopy look on his face and began to chirp the opening lines of "I Really Like Him."

"Alec, you never take anything seriously."

"As the one and only Lotte Lenya so aptly put it in the song of the same title, 'So What?' "

"Well maybe this will cheer you up." And I told him how I'd used his idea at the store, and how it had gotten bigger and bigger, and the boss was so pleased he gave me a raise. "And it's all thanks to you, Alec."

But he wasn't happy. "Sure, everything is thanks to me. You're a success, Harold's a success, and where am I? The assistant manager at the record store quit today. Just watch who gets the job. Probably that dope Bernie, after *I* taught him how to inventory the whole damned classical section."

"Sorry, Alec. I just thought it'd make you feel better."

"Sure. Thanks."

"Thank *you*."

He smiled at me. "Feel like some brandy?"

I had to admit it, I kind of liked Alec, when he wasn't with those friends of his. He was easy to talk to, especially when I'd had a bad day or was tired after work. If I told Tony about something that had happened to piss me off, he'd just say, "Yeah, it's tough, but your job's a piece of cake compared to waiting tables." But Alec understood. If I told him, say, about some dope who spent an hour looking without buying so much as a sweat band, he'd know what I meant, or some creep who'd copy down all our prices so he could run over to Sears to see if he could save fifty cents, Alec had seen it all. He could do these imitations of customers that were really a scream. While we were drinking our brandy, I asked him why, with all his talent, he never tried out for any of the local theater productions.

"Too nerve-wracking. Zero in the self-confidence department. Besides, do I look like a leading man?"

"There are other parts."

"I suppose. But I'd still have to listen to these amateur directors who don't know what they're doing. There's a theater group downtown led by some prissy old queen — this guy is to directors what Harold is to reviewers. Worse than that, he thinks Harold is a pro! His idea of biting satire was *Doonesbury*. Or the guy who used to direct at the university, before this new man came. Did *Hello, Dolly!* two years out of five. Considered *Pippin* a theatrical breakthrough, called *Snoopy* the state of the art. And try something new? Maybe a show that didn't quite make it on Broadway but still had something to offer? 'Jupiter forbid!' "

"Then maybe you could do something behind the scenes, be a director yourself."

"Sure, walk in and say, 'Look, you idiot, you're butchering this show. Listen to me, I know how to do it. After all, I sell records. Not well enough to be assistant manager, but take it from me, I know my stuff!' "

"You know something, Alec, you depress me. You're a real downer."

"And I suppose your life is a bed of roses?"

"We weren't discussing me."

"No, but we should. You and your muscles, flexing this, measuring that, trying on those little shirts to see how they show you off. Don't deny it. I see you do it in front of the mirror."

"Now listen, I told you not to get any ideas. So just stop watching me."

"Stop leaving your door open."

"Stop spying."

"Stop whining."

"Shut up."

"Fuck you."

Did I say Alec was easy to talk to?

SCENE X

The Gay Life

Beating off may be OK, but not when it threatens to become a way of life, and a guy reaches a point where his ego needs some stroking along with everything else. Besides, there's just so much you can do with two hands, some spit, and a cake of soap. So a couple of nights, after the store closed, I drifted by that bar, the Alamo. It's an ordinary looking place, college kids don't pay much attention to decor as long as there's beer on tap. The decorations consist of a few "Remember the Alamo" banners, a ratty old deer's head with a cowboy hat stuck on one antler, and a motheaten coonskin cap with a sign that says "Davy Crockett slept here." That's it for atmosphere. A few years ago, Tony told me, someone sent the bar's name to one of those gay guides, which listed it as having a "western" ambience, so every once in a while some tourist or big-city faggot comes to check the place out, all done up in cowboy gear, boots, hat, even chaps. The locals always get a good laugh out of that, Tony said. Tony knew a lot about goings-on in town; I guess he picked it up at the restaurant, since we hardly were regulars at the place.

Anyhow, what with the college crowd going back to preppy clothes, the bar doesn't have any particular look. Which suits me, since I don't cultivate any one style. Tony used to call it eclectic chic, a term he got out of one of those grooming books, the kind that are really intended to show off great-looking guys in their underwear. But I like to think of myself as ''athletic casual,'' since I try to project my interest in fitness. So I usually wear running shoes with Levis or cords and a shirt with some athletic company's logo; luckily I can get a discount down at the store. I'm not a fanatic when it comes to clothes, but a guy does have to know what's current on the fashion scene, whether collars are getting wider, pants tight or cut full. I keep up on the catalogs, watch the ads, catch GQ at the gym. After all, I face the public every day at work and I have to look my best. Not that I can afford all the stuff I'd like to have, but face it, those ads have the best-looking guys you'll see anywhere, showing everything they can get away with this side of *Playgirl.*

So I wasn't worried about dressing for my first solo trip to the bar; I figured I could just wear some of my workout clothes, a tight T-shirt would wow them. The real problem was getting up the nerve to go in. Like I said, the Alamo doesn't start getting gay till about 11. It closes at one, so you don't have much time to make it or break it. Of course that didn't matter when I stopped by with Tony, but I had noticed that the place could be unpredictable. Some nights it's as if this signal goes out to all the gay guys, and no one shows up; the next night it'll be mobbed. The first time I dropped in, around 10:30, there was no one there, and I wondered if maybe some new place had opened. I hung around forty-five minutes, then gave up. But the next time, there were a good thirty guys. I didn't recognize anyone, not that I'd expected to, and I hoped they didn't recognize me, either. At least I'd be a new face and therefore in big demand. Problem was, all the people there seemed to know each other, and I ended up standing at the bar staring into my beer. I caught a couple of guys looking my way and glanced back at them, but they turned to their friends and didn't look again. I knew it was silly, just nerves, but I got the funny feeling people were talking about me, looking over at me on the sly, which made me uncomfortable. I didn't stay very long.

The next time I stopped by there was a decent crowd. I got my beer and moved to a corner where I could look over the room. Well, who should I find right beside me but the Birdies — Tom and Randy — with a few others of their sort. So I went back to the bar and kind of hunched over so they wouldn't notice me. After a few minutes, Randy came over to buy another round.

''Well, well, well. Will you look who's slumming. Hello, Joe.''

''Hi.''

''Alone?''

''Looks like it.''

''Feel free to join us in the back.'' He gave me this coy look and a big smile. ''Don't worry, I wouldn't *dream* of doing anything to embarrass you.'' Except that while he was saying it, he was running his hand up my thigh. I could have killed him.

I grabbed my beer and slunk off to a table in front. After a couple of minutes I noticed a guy looking me over. He seemed OK, friendly, even if I could tell he didn't work out, so I nodded at him. Next thing I knew he'd picked up his glass and was sitting next to me.

''Hi. My name's Andy.''

''Joe.''

''Hi, Joe. Say, you're Alec's roommate, aren't you?''

I could feel myself turn red. How the hell did he know that? ''For the time being. I'm still looking for a place.''

''He's really something, isn't he?''

I couldn't argue with that, but I didn't know what this guy meant when he said it. ''How so?''

He shook his head. "Biggest one I've ever seen. But then, I never did see Tony's."

"What the hell are you talking about, and leave Tony out of it."

"Touchy, touchy." He picked up his beer and went over to a group of guys. I could see him whispering to them, then they all laughed.

Needless to say I cut out of there pretty fast. I was breathing hard; it felt like someone had punched me in the gut. Who was that little bastard, and how did he know all that, about me and Alec, and Tony? And why did he think I'd know how big Alec was? I walked around the block a few times to cool off before I went home. Alec was lying on the sofa, waving his hands in the air to conduct the overture to *Candide* playing on his stereo. I figured he was depressed; he always played that show when he needed cheering up. I grunted good night and went to bed. I was in no mood to listen to anyone else's problems. I lay in bed and tried to forget about the Birdies and Andy and all those fruity little fems. I'd never go back to the Alamo. The last thing I remembered hearing before I finally fell asleep was "Glitter and Be Gay."

Having ruled out the bar, I was back at square one, so I decided I'd have to try a little harder with Jerry. After all, I was about killing myself with those weights just to spend time near him, but the thrill of holding his wrists was wearing a little thin, and when my mind wandered I'd find myself staring at his thighs and crotch to see if I could make out the bulge of his basket. I was afraid I'd give myself away before I was absolutely sure about him. He *was* friendly, always greeted me by saying "there's my man!" And did he ever have clothes — things I'd think twice about wearing in public. One day he came in sporting shiny black pants that stuck to him like a suntan.

''Like these?'' he asked, twisting his leg so I could see his hamstrings flex through the fabric.

''Nice, real nice. What are they for, skiing?''

''Nah. Bike racing. Italian bike racing pants.'' He rubbed his hand along his groin. ''See, no seams. You don't get chafed. Wait till you see my other pair. Turquoise.'' He gave me a big smile, and I thought he might have winked. Those pants sure captured my attention that day. I kept thinking how sexy he'd look with a hard-on showing through them, and I almost popped out of my own shorts.

That's how Jerry could be. Friendly, downright seductive. Problem was, he was the same, more or less, with everyone. He loved to tell jokes in the locker room, always had a crowd around him. Some of them were funny, even provocative, like when he asked why a dog licks its own dick. ''Because he can,'' he said, grinning at me. But some of his jokes were kind of sicko, especially his sheep jokes. ''What's the difference between a woman and a sheep?'' He'd wait till he had everyone's attention. ''A sheep won't do the dishes.'' The guys in the locker room thought that was a scream. I didn't — I'd heard enough jokes like that back on the farm. Of course, we didn't raise sheep, just cows. I had heard some guys say nothing could match the grip of a suckling calf, so I guess that's what sheep farmers joke about. Jerry was encouraged by the response he was getting, so pretty soon he was going on about the farmer who counted sheep when he wanted to stay up.

Sometimes I thought he told these jokes because that's the way guys are, in a locker room, friendly, sociable, like me keeping my eye on the ball scores in case anyone asked. And sometimes I thought maybe he didn't really like women or was turned off by all those rockhard girls out there pumping iron along with the rest of us. And sometimes I even thought, when he looked at me and grinned, that he was doing this for me, to get me to laugh, to tell me that women were something to joke about, but not what he was really interested in. But he sure loved an audience, and as long as he kept all those naked guys bent over laughing, I figured I might as well join in the fun.

Then he wore the turquoise pants. "Just for you, Joe, my man, I knew you'd like 'em." That day I left only one shower head between him and me instead of the usual two or three, you know, because guys are careful not to get too close to each other, and I took a little longer soaping my dick, just to see if there'd be any reaction from him. He just took his shower and smiled at me through the steam. But then he said we ought to get together for breakfast some morning after our workout. Sounds good, I told him, and we agreed maybe the next week. Finally, a step in the right direction. And if I didn't know for sure what would come of it, I did know one thing — I'd better stop soaping my dick because it was starting to feel real good.

Alec had been right about Harold making up with him. They were back on good terms and went out to a couple of local plays that Harold had to review for the paper. Alec came home one night from an amateur production of *Gypsy* singing "Little Lamb" in a warbling falsetto.

"How was it?"

"Awful."

"I suppose Harold's going to savage it in his review?"

"Of course not. He never says anything bad about local efforts. That's his public out there. He'll say that Mama Rose was loaded with stage presence. What he won't say is that she had no talent. The chorus will be described as 'enthusiastic' meaning they couldn't even fall down in unison, and the striptease will be called 'discreet,' which is to say she was smart enough to keep her body covered at all times. I dictated the review to him on the way home."

"I don't see why you don't let him do it himself and show everyone what a fool he is."

"If he did it himself, it'd be just like an 'emotion paper' from his class. He'd tell how he felt; that's not criticism. For the little it's worth, people might as well get something with a trace of substance."

"Then write it yourself."

He shook his head. "No one really wants to hear bad things about a hometown production. Harold's love 'em style waters down the criticism and we get a nice homogenized product for local consumption."

"And Harold is a star."

"Let's not get into that again. Why should they hire me? This way I'm the power behind the throne."

"Yeah, well the next time you're near the throne, give it a good flush"

Alec laughed. "You know, Harold can be very entertaining. And he doesn't take himself too seriously, so it's hard to stay mad at him. If you'd give him half a chance. . . ."

Alec hadn't been in such good spirits lately, feeling sorry for himself and worrying about who was going to be promoted as his new boss at the record store, so I decided not to argue with him. Besides, he had the munchies and was taking out the last seafood crepe left over from dinner along with two plates and a couple of wine glasses to finish off the bottle of Riesling.

"I hear you've been out on the town yourself," he said when he put the food in front of me. "Almost a regular at the Alamo."

"Only a few times."

"Any luck?"

"Didn't hang around long enough." Alec had this habit of asking me questions I knew he already had the answers to. He'd play the innocent, but I knew damn well his fluttery friends must have filled him in on my every move. "I wish Tom and Randy would mind their own business."

"How so? Did someone dare speak to you? In a public place?"

"Lay off, Alec. I mean telling stories. Talking to strangers about me."

"Like who?"

"Some little creep named Andy."

"A-a-a-h, Andy. Haven't seen him in weeks."

"Well he knew all about me living here and jumped to a lot of conclusions. And even had the nerve to mention Tony."

"The gall!"

"I'm not kidding, Alec. You wouldn't think it was so funny if you knew what he said about you."

"What?"

"Nothing. Forget it." I could play this game as well as he could.

"Joe!"

"He said you had the biggest cock he's ever seen."

Alec clutched his chest then put the back of his hand to his forehead. "My secret is out! Listen to this song, Joe. It's called 'I Have a Noble Cock.' " He started crooning in a deep baritone. And while I'd have to admit the words were pretty racy, I wasn't about to let him distract me.

"Go ahead, sing your songs. But I'd think it would bother you, people talking like that."

"Puh-leeze! If I'm not known for anything else in this town, I'm at least famous for my endowments. Wanna peek?"

"Alec, I told you . . . ."

"I'm just kidding. I've made it with Andy, so what's the big deal? I haven't been to the Alamo in ages. Let me know if you want to go back, I'll introduce you around."

I already knew as many of that crowd as I intended to. But Alec was taking the walnut rum raisin ice cream out of the freezer, so I let it drop. I knew one way to change the subject — I asked him if he knew any show tunes with the words "ice cream" in them. He launched into a number from *She Loves Me.* He was hardly into his medley before I'd finished the carton.

SCENE XI

Something for the Boys

I hadn't forgotten what Jerry had said about the two of us going out for breakfast, and I kept waiting for him to bring it up again. After a week and a half, I finally reminded him. "We'll have to put it on hold, my man," he told me; he had to go out of town for a while, to a convention. So now I didn't even have my workouts to look forward to, or that breakfast. On top of which, without him there to spot me, I cut my hand on a rough spot on a barbell. I didn't even realize it till I saw blood on a twenty-pound plate. Scared me so bad I dropped the damn thing on my foot, and it was all I could do to keep from screaming. But that's not something you do at the gym, so I hobbled into the locker room and began to rethink this free-weight business. I mean, this was exactly the sort of thing I'd been afraid of. I'd keep it up just till I'd snared Jerry.

Jerry was gone temporarily, but my other problem looked like it was becoming permanent. I'd made beating off a real art, God knows I'd been getting enough practice. When Alec wasn't home, I used the full-length mirror behind his bedroom door. I could take my time and watch myself from different angles; then I discovered I could put a shaving mirror on the floor between my legs, and all sorts of new vantage points opened themselves up. I thought it was very creative, on my part. But then, I'd been feeling pretty artistic lately, what with the job I'd been doing on the displays down at the store. Creative or not, beating off was still beating off, and my dick, being tender like the rest of me, needed something wet and warm and without fingernails. The more I thought about it, the more my mind kept going back to that campus men's room. I'd vowed never to go near it again, since it wasn't exclusive, and people knew me now — if anyone saw me down there, it'd be all over the Alamo in no time. Besides, since I'd become a weight lifter and had perfected my already great body, I wouldn't want to give it away to some unworthy guy in a john. Still, I kept thinking, I could be very careful and selective, and maybe, just maybe, it was time for the return of the blond phantom.

I didn't rush into this, of course. I checked things out. Hung around the corridor by the stairs, pretending I was reading notices on the bulletin board, but really watching who came and went. Just to make sure it was the number one place for young guys and hadn't been taken over by old men from town. I saw a couple of nice ones go down there, too, but they were sure to have seen me, so I couldn't follow them if I was going to avoid blowing my cover. I waited till I knew it was empty and headed on down.

The first thing that hit me was the smell on the stairs, the old familiar combination of disinfectant and piss. Then the place itself, the three old ceramic urinals, the cracked sink that still dripped, and those three dark stalls with the scratched-up wooden doors and the marble partitions that stopped almost a foot and a half above the floor. It felt smaller than I'd remembered and smelled worse when I was down there, but a funny feeling came over me, a surge of adrenalin, or maybe it was hormones, a reminder of how exciting the john had seemed in the beginning, the thrill of hearing footsteps scraping down the stairs, the racing of my pulse when a guy came into the stall next to me.

A glimpse of ankle or an inch of shin seems real sexy, when it's all you can see. No doubt about it, I'd come home again.

The peep holes were still there, only bigger now. Someone had drawn a big black circle and written "glory hole here", then scratched at the marble. But there was no hole, which was just as well; it's harder to stay hidden when you have to keep an eye on a glory hole. I'd only planned to look around and leave, but there was so much graffiti, I sat in all three stalls and read everything, the titillation mounting from one description to the next. Not a word about the blond mystery man, though, which was a little disappointing, but it'd been over a year now and I could start again with a new crowd, maybe even meet someone like Tony.

I was so engrossed in reading the walls that when I heard footsteps rushing down the stairs, I barely managed to slam shut the stall door I'd had to leave open a crack to let the light in. I was so excited I almost forgot to stick toilet paper in the hole. He was wearing dark slacks and penny loafers — not a clear sign about his age — and he didn't waste any time before he was tapping away. I hung down to see what I could of his leg. Luckily he was in the middle stall, which got the most light from the overhead bulb. The first thing I noticed was his belt buckle. Now I'd seen that kind of buckle before, with a silver dollar embedded in it, even knew a few stores where you could buy one. But I also knew that Randy had one just like it. Suddenly I was paralyzed with fear — what if Randy or Tom or that creep Andy came down there? They were hardly what you'd call discreet, any one of them, and would probably do whatever they had to in order to get a look at me. So my cock, which had been begging me to free it from my still unzipped pants, did a quick swan dive; I put my coat over my face and made a run for it.

This new fear haunted me as I ran up the stairs to the

snack bar, but after I'd sat down with a cup of coffee and had a look around, I realized my worries were silly. I didn't know a soul in the whole place. There must have been seven or eight thousand guys at the university, at least a few hundred of them gay, and the chance of my meeting someone I knew down there was pretty remote. Besides, I remembered that I'd heard the Birdies making fun of the tea room. They had this friend, some guy I'd never met, who they called ''Stewie sewerpants'' because he went down to that john. And the guys who did go down there were usually uptight about being seen anyway, not the types who'd be regulars at the Alamo. So by the time I'd finished my coffee, I decided I had nothing to worry about. I was mad at myself for letting my foolish fears make me pass up what might have been a great chance. So I tiptoed back down the stairs. Just as I stepped into the john, there was a loud rustling and scraping of shoes and shifting of bodies, and I barely glimpsed two guys getting up from the floor. No sooner had I ducked into the empty stall than I could hear them tearing up toilet paper — they were exchanging notes — then both were out of there in a flash, leaving me alone with the graffiti and a mental picture of the fun they must have been having. Boy, was I mad! That was something else I'd forgotten about the tea room, how damn frustrating it could be when you missed a good shot.

I kept telling myself I'd be better off if I didn't get back into the tea room habit, and I managed to stay away for a whole day. But, I thought, why not, it'd just be till Jerry got back to town and we met for breakfast and laid everything out in the open. Besides, college guys were likely to be healthy, not the sort to mess around in unsafe places in the city. So the next day I found myself outwaiting an old man and then a fatty, which almost made me late for work. I thought about writing ''the phantom has returned'' on the wall, but I couldn't get my pen to write on the marble.

The following day I resolved not to spend more than a half hour down there. Fortunately, someone showed up a couple of minutes after I sat down. Looked OK for starters, cords and sneakers, and his calf was hairy. I was pretty hard up at that point, so when this hand came under the partition I moved over and let him stroke the back of my thigh. Then I reached under and felt his hardon, which was thick, if not too long. Some guys feel a lot better than they actually look, so I figured I'd better not go much further if I didn't want to be disappointed. He had on a leather cock ring that tightened around his balls and made them like rocks. I decided he'd do, if I could get him to suck me, so when he got down on his knees, I squatted and faced the partition. He grabbed my dick and sized it up. I could hear him breathing hard.

"Oh, my G-o-o-od," he moaned, and "Oh, my *God*!" I thought. I'd know that whine anywhere. I had half a mind to march over and give that idiot Harold a good talking to, him a professor and celebrity and all, down on all fours on a tea room floor. How could he! So I stood up and tried to shove my hard-on into my bikini briefs and zip up without mangling myself. And I'll be damned if that asshole, still reaching for me, didn't say, "Ten bucks! I'll give you ten bucks if you stay!"

I was out of there before he was even off his knees and was grossed out enough to want to barf. How's that for an emotion, Harold? And to think he'd touched me! I'd have to go home and shower. And offering me ten bucks! Twenty would barely have put him in the ball park.

It wasn't till later that the possibility struck me: suppose Harold had seen me? I kept telling myself he couldn't have. I *knew* he was still getting up from the floor when I left, but just suppose he'd seen me through the crack in the door. How could I face him? Who would he tell? I couldn't get the awful thought from my mind for the rest of the day. Even work didn't distract me.

"Anything wrong, Joe?" Judy asked me after I'd missed the chance to talk a customer into a big sale.

"Not really. Just thinking something over."

"Well, I'm here if ever you want to talk. I was brought up Catholic, so confessions come natural to me."

"Who's going to do the confessing?"

She waved her hand. "Oh, we all have our little secrets."

Now what did she mean by that? Did she think I wanted to tell her I was gay, one queer to another? She'd been getting awfully friendly lately, trying to help me out with the store displays, offering to cover for me if I felt like taking a break. But I didn't want to get too close to her. I could just imagine her knowing smiles every time I waited on a good-looking guy. The next thing I knew she'd been trying to get me to join some political group. Those lesbians are always joining groups.

Luckily Bud saved me; he needed me in the back to help unload a delivery of running pants. He even asked if I had any ideas about displaying them. I thought maybe we could straighten coat hangers and stick them into the pants, then bend them to look like running legs — our own marathon, right across the front of the store. He loved it.

"Hey, Bud, you seen those Italian bike racing pants?"

"Nope. New?"

"Yeah. No seams, so they don't chafe. Great colors. I think they're gonna be big."

"I'll call my distributor. Thanks for the tip."

Just then Judy turned up next to me with a big smile. "Scoring a few points with the boss, are you, Joe?"

What'd she think, I had the hots for him? "Just doing my job."

"Keep up the good work," she laughed. And damn if that bitch didn't pat my behind.

"Lay off, Judy, I don't like that."

"I think I know what you like," she said with a grin. "We'll talk about it one of these days. When Bud's not around."

Up till then, the store had been my refuge, the one place where I could forget my other problems. Not any more, not since Judy was on my trail. I kept thinking of what grandma used to say: "God gave us honey, but He sent the bees down with it." With Judy buzzing around, it was just a matter of time till I got stung.

SCENE XII

Les Misérables

I thought when I got rid of Tony that all sorts of possibilities would open up. But the one possibility I hadn't imagined was the mess I found myself in. And Judy was the least of it. I couldn't bring myself to go to the Alamo, I was afraid of who I might run into in the tea room; Jerry was still out of town, and I dreaded my next meeting with Harold.

On top of all that, Alec wasn't around much, so I didn't even have him to talk to when I needed him. The Birdies had both gotten parts in the university spring musical, and Alec had started going up with them to watch the rehearsals. He was reluctant at first, but apparently Harold told him he'd OK'd it with the new director. I could see Harold throwing his weight around, trying to impress the new kid on the block.

"How's the show going?" I asked Alec the next time we were together for dinner.

"Pretty good. Harold's doing a publicity piece for the paper. He introduced me to the director."

"The guy Tom thinks is always pawing him?"

"He wishes. Actually, this guy, everyone calls him Kelly, is doing a good job."

"You mean Harold's going to write a rave review and mean it for once?"

Alec laughed. I had a feeling he didn't think I was all that smart, so I liked it when I was able to make him laugh.

"I suppose what I mean is that I've talked to him a few times, and he seems interested in what I have to say. I told him that every time I heard that score, I pictured in my head how I'd stage one of the songs. I thought he was humoring me by even listening to me, but what do you know? The next day he tried my idea."

"Maybe this is your big break."

"Sure. Kid, you're going out a store clerk and coming back a star."

"You're putting yourself down again. You should have more confidence in yourself. You can do anything you put your mind to."

That was his cue for a medley of "can" songs: "Anything You Can Do," "Anyone Can Whistle," "Who Can? You can!," "He Can Do It," "I Can." I knew this conversation wasn't going anywhere, and when he started on "Can-Can" I couldn't keep from laughing. I had to admit it to myself, I was glad he was around. Just to have someone to talk to, to laugh with, even fight with. Not to mention being served a hot meal.

After dinner we watched a movie on TV. "*Carousel* is my absolute favorite R and H," he said, "even if they did water it down a little, clean up a few lyrics. But then, what musical hasn't suffered in the film version? And the 'If I Loved You' sequence really is beautiful."

I hadn't intended to join him, but I didn't have anything else to do. The picture was as sappy as I'd expected, but even so, I couldn't help wiping away a tear at the end. And besides, we knocked off half a bottle of brandy.

"So how's it going at the store?" I asked him when the flick was over. "Do you know who your new boss is yet?"

"No. There's all sorts of talk going around. That they're bringing in someone new, some hotshot kid with a business degree, I suppose. 'New ideas.' Even rumors about a shake-up of employees. I'd rather not even think about it. What's new at your place? I noticed the windows look better."

"Yeah. I'm kind of in charge of them. It's funny how one idea leads to another."

"I know. I watch them rehearse that show up on campus, and I get all sorts of ideas. I don't say anything, though. I'm lucky the director even lets me watch." He sighed. We stared into our glasses. I guess the brandy gave me the nerve to ask my next question.

"Alec?"

"Yeah?"

"What do you do about sex?"

"What?"

"You heard me."

"Is that an offer?"

"Alec!"

"I know, I know, I'm not 'getting any ideas.' What brings this up, or is it the alcohol talking?"

"It's just that, well, I'm kind of up a tree. You know, I don't know anyone or how to meet anyone."

"Yeah, well I know everyone and I'm up the same tree. You're not missing much."

"So you're not . . . seeing anybody?"

"Nah. I used to go out a lot, the bar, parties. Oh, I never missed a chance — 'The Life of the Party' might as well have been my theme song. You may not believe this, but there was a time, any new face in town, he wasn't in with the In Crowd till he'd made it with old Alec."

"But not anymore?"

"I guess I've outgrown it all. These college guys, away from home for the first time, they're looking for fun, not a relationship. I've had enough fun. You lose too much sleep. Besides, I'm healthy and I plan to stay that way. Why are we talking about this?''

''I was just curious. It's not like you're old or ugly or anything.''

''Look, I just got fed up with . . .with . . .being used.''

''You don't mean . . . .''

''So I have a big cock, OK? That's not all there is to me. Sure, it was great for a while. I'd see a guy look my way, someone would whisper in his ear, look down at my pants, and the next thing I knew, we were on our way. But then I started getting invitations to the men's room for a quickie, even weird phone calls. 'Hi, my friend told me about you. Can we get together?' I mean, who needs it?''

''Look, I'm sorry.''

''No reason for you to be sorry. It's no wonder there are so many stupid pricks in this town — you are what you eat. So you're not getting any, either?'' I shook my head and he laughed. ''Well, here we sit, the biggest cock and the hottest bod in town, just a couple of wall flowers. 'Nobody's heart belongs to me, heigh ho, who cares?' '' He reached for the brandy bottle and emptied it into our two glasses. ''What should we drink to? Purity? Celibacy?''

''How about to finding two great guys?''

''We *are* two great guys. Think about it.'' Then he was off, trilling ''My White Knight'' in a high soprano. He raised his drink and smiled at me. ''Not a bad Barbara Cook, huh, Joe? Wait for my last note. I just might break these glasses.''

SCENE XIII

One Mo' Time

The hottest bod in town was cooling off quickly. With nothing to occupy me, I kept thinking of Jerry, and I was eager for his return to the gym. He'd told me he'd be out of town for a week, and I spent that week remembering how he looked in the shower, how he felt when I was helping him with the weights, how he smiled, how he filled out those Italian racing pants. I was really looking forward to that breakfast we'd planned when he got back, and I tried to imagine how it would go, how we'd start by talking about our training, then make a few vague, tentative remarks. He might tell me another of his dumb jokes, and I'd laugh and point out that a guy could get the impression Jerry didn't have much use for women. He'd tell me how they did nothing for him, and our knees would touch under the table, a casual brush at first, then a noticeable pressure. He'd come up with a reason to invite me back to his place, like maybe he had a pair of racing pants that didn't quite fit him but would be perfect on me. I could see the two of us pulling on a couple of pairs of those pants, better yet, pulling them off.

Needless to say, I wanted to make sure I saw him as soon as he got back to town, so I spent a lot of time at the gym that week. I had to— since I'd dropped that weight on my foot, I wasn't able to go running, and I was putting in my miles on the stationery bike. Early the next week I started asking around if anyone had seen him yet, but if he was back, he was making himself scarce, so I sat there, pedaling away, fantasizing about me and Jerry doing all the things I'd done with Tony and maybe even a few more, and pretty soon I realized I'd slowed my pace to where my legs were hardly moving and I was getting a hard-on. Then I had to pedal a lot faster to get rid of it. I pedaled so hard that I wore the skin raw inside my thigh — I guess I should have been wearing a pair of seamless racing pants.

I'd been counting on Jerry's return to improve my mood, but his continued absence only made things worse, things like meeting Harold for the first time after our encounter. I was nervous about it, and I listened for his voice on my way up the stairs every night. Sometimes I almost convinced myself that it wasn't really him I'd run into in the tea room, but I could still hear the whine that told me it couldn't have been anyone else. Once, just as I was putting my key in the door, I heard him inside, so I turned around and went out for a cup of coffee. Another time I'd already opened the door before I heard his giggle, so I did an about-face and ran for the stairs just as Alec stuck his head out to see what was up. Then I heard a commercial and realized it was just the TV. Alec seemed skeptical when I told him I was running up and down the stairs for exercise.

The inevitable finally happened the following weekend. I'd heard the Birdies chirping away and a record in the background, so I didn't know Harold was there until I was already inside. Tom and Randy were fussing about some cast changes in that show they were doing and pestering Harold to swear he'd mention their names in his review. I tried to sneak by them to my room.

"Joe, wait a minute!" Harold called to me; I froze. "Joe, you big beautiful hunk, save me from these vultures."

"You can take care of yourself, Harold." I looked

down at his feet; he was wearing the same sneakers he'd had on in the john. I shivered.

"I'd much rather you took care of me, handsome. Or we could take care of you. What do you say, Tom, Randy? Let's all gang up on Joe. He could use some warming up. We could have our way with him."

"What is your way, Harold?" I asked him.

"Any way I can, beautiful."

Even it if means paying for it, I thought to myself. Just then Alec came out of the kitchen with a big bowl of popcorn. "Harold, control yourself. Stop picking on Joe."

"*Picking* on him? I'm *throwing* myself at him." Then to me, "Hey, kid, wanna see your name in the papers?" That set the Birdies off again, so I was able to grab a handful of popcorn and get to my room. I figured I'd passed the first trial, but maybe he was waiting to get me alone. Maybe he'd been playing for time, so he could check out *my* shoes. Maybe he planned to make his pitch later, you know, like blackmail me, I make it with him or he'd talk. Maybe that's what he meant by my name in the papers. No, I was just letting my imagination run at full speed. Harold wasn't fast enough to keep up. At least I didn't think so. I'd better play it safe, be nicer to him, at least as nice as I could stand to be. I sat in my room and brooded and wondered what Alec did to get that great cheesy taste in the popcorn.

A couple of days later Jerry still hadn't turned up at the gym, so I decided the odds of meeting Harold again were a million to one, and besides, I knew what his shoes looked like. I'd be careful, I told myself as I tiptoed down the stairs to the tea room. I'd make sure I got a good look through the peep hole before I gave myself away down there. Luck was with me. There was someone in the middle stall; I could grab the one closest to the door without having to pass in front of him. The hole was small on this side, and every time I took a look, I saw an eye staring back. The guy was wearing running shoes, a top of the line model that looked like they'd really been run in. So I knew right off it wasn't Tom or Randy or Harold or anyone like that.

Since we'd already eyeballed each other, we didn't waste much time with the preliminaries. He was down on his knees in no time. Looked good, too, great cock, tight balls, like two fuzzy apricots. I was still a little nervous about being down there and needed some coaxing to get it up, but he was reaching for me eagerly. The middle stall, where he was, got the most light, and he kept pulling me toward him so he could take it all in. Then we started to get into it, reaching up to feel each other's chest and all, and I was wedged right under there in a good position to get sucked. Then I'll be damned if he didn't just freeze up. Pushed me back, pulled on his pants, buckled up and disappeared.

Now you meet all sorts of weirdoes in the tea room — guys who take forty minutes before they'll make a move, guys who want to watch you beat off, or want you to watch them. I've sat for hours in the middle stall with a guy on each side, neither one of them so much as moving a toe. And I've been stuck in an end stall while some creep sits in the middle like a stone, determined to keep the two guys next to him from getting together. I mean, I've seen it all, a variety of sickies who seem to enjoy preventing other guys from having a healthy, normal quickie. But why this one ran like that, when we'd been getting along so well, I just couldn't figure. So I moved into his stall, to picture what it must have been like from over there, did he maybe see something or hear someone, or what? But everything seemed to check out, so I decided I'd better take a good look at myself — did I have lint stuck to my cock, something that didn't look right? I examined myself all over, then spread my legs wide. Suddenly I knew: that damn irritation I'd gotten on the stationery bike, this big red welt, looking for all the world like some horrible rash all inside my thigh.

Goddam! If only I'd remembered it, I would've been careful not to push myself so far under. If only I'd had the middle stall, and he'd been on the dark side. If only he hadn't been in such a hurry and we'd written notes, I could've explained it to him. Damn, damn. That's how that tea room could get to you. And he'd been a real catch.

I was all wilted up by now, not even in the mood to beat off. Then I heard footsteps on the stairs — I'd still have a chance if I was careful about that welt. But the shoes were black wingtips and the pants gray wool, and you don't have to give me a birth certificate for me to spot an old fart, so I made a run for it. Which wasn't easy, since my foot still hurt. I was falling apart.

SCENE XIV

Mr. Wonderful

Now I was absolutely sure Jerry said he was going to be gone for a week — I could remember every word of our last conversation. But it was over two weeks before he finally turned up at the gym. A wave of relief came over me, like things were going to turn themselves around at last. He seemed glad to see me.

"There's my man! All right, Joe, how ya doing?"

"Great, Jer, great. Good to see you're back." What I wanted to say was good to see your back, your front, your thighs, your dick and let's hit the showers.

He wiggled his shoulder to loosen up, making all his muscles jump to attention. "Man, I'm outta shape. It's been a while. Come on, buddy, let's get this workout going."

So we fell back into the old routine. I hadn't done my lifting with much enthusiasm while he was away, in fact I'd gone back to the regular Nautilus machines, so I felt a lot of the old pains waiting to creep back in. But it was worth the pain, because Jerry never left my side, talking a blue streak, fillling me in on this convention he'd gone to, in Las Vegas. A couple of other guys started listening in, and Jerry got warmed up, like he did when he had an audience. Began describing the nightclub shows he'd seen in Vegas.

"Dozens of naked titties, you don't know where to look first. Just follow the bouncing balls. Damned if I didn't get hypnotized. Clap your hands three times and there's no telling what I'll do!'' He winked at me. ''Wild place, Las Vegas. They've set off so many nuclear bombs there, the hookers don't have to stand under street lights — they glow in the dark! And they got these Basque sheepherders, came over from Europe — heard American sheep were better looking. Turns out someone pulled the wool over their eyes. That's the sheepherders' expression for cunnilingus.'' His eyes twinkled; he was on a roll. ''Nevada — where the men are men, the women are men, and the sheep run scared.''

Needless to say, he had the crowd in stitches. Not exactly the reunion I'd had in mind, but he did seem to look my way every time he got to a punch line. ''Really, though,'' he was saying, ''I was with this great bunch of guys. Got bombed every night, did the craziest things.''

When we were finally alone, I asked him, ''So that's why you were gone so long, huh? Partying it up?''

''Truth is, Joe, I've been back almost a week. Just couldn't bring myself to work out. Had to get some sleep, clean out my system. Not that I haven't been lifting a few brews, a little tail of the dog. Been hanging around up by the campus. Things are just the same up there, like when I was in school. Crazy place, the Alamo.''

If he hadn't grabbed my arms I'd've dropped the barbell I was pressing right onto my stomach. Here he was, telling me he'd been at the Alamo, and I'd been avoiding the damn bar for weeks. ''So you hang out at the Alamo?'' I asked him, when I'd gotten my balance back.

''I've been known to spend a few hours there once in a while. Oh, I know what they say about it,'' he leaned closer to me and lowered his voice, ''you know, that the guys who stop in there are a little. . . .'' He wiggled his hand in a doubtful gesture. ''But it's still the most interesting place in town. I'm willing to bet you've been there yourself.''

''Sure, I stop in now and then. Doesn't everybody?''

I didn't want to lose my momentum just when things were getting good. "So what d'ya say, Jer, maybe we can get together some time. At the Alamo, for a beer."

"You got it, my man. Any time."

"How about tomorrow night?"

He shook his head. "Can't make it tomorrow."

"Maybe the day after?"

"Let's see. No, that's bad, too. Truth is, Joe, I'm so far behind at work I've got to put in some extra hours. The company paid for the week in Vegas, not for the week I took off when I got back."

I couldn't very well pull out a calendar and mark down his first free night. "Well, sometime, then," was all I could say.

"Sure. As soon as I'm caught up."

There were a few other guys in the locker room when we went to shower, so we didn't say much after that. But as he was leaving, he aimed his finger at me. "But I *can* make it for breakfast. Haven't forgotten that, my man. One of these days real soon."

Of course the first night I was off I went up to the Alamo, early, around nine. It was full of college kids and a few older guys trying to hit on coeds. They were all laughing and talking, and I felt pretty alone. I positioned myself so I could watch the door. If Jerry came in with other guys, I wanted him to see me and make the first move. After a while, my foot fell asleep, so I had to turn my back to the door and watch in the mirror behind the bar. I kept remembering what he'd said, about doing crazy things when he'd been drinking, so maybe I'd be better off it we met here and lifted a few than waste a lot of time over breakfast. I kept my eyes glued to the mirror, but the place was so crowded I had to keep moving from side to side to avoid this girl who was blocking my view. Our eyes met a few times, and finally she came over to me, and right out, she said, "Hi, I couldn't help notice you watching me in the mirror. My name is Donna." I blushed and mumbled something about having to meet a friend. I guess that's what they call the new woman. I wish the gay guys had her guts.

I beat a hasty retreat and found myself out on the sidewalk wondering what to do next. It wouldn't be too much longer before the crowd started to change. But then I saw that creep Andy coming up the street, which didn't leave me much choice but to go home and think about whether I'd try this again the next night. In fact, I tried the next two nights. But I never did see Jerry, and three more girls tried to pick me up. The third night it snowed, and Alec was making hot mulled cider to go with a spice cake he'd whipped up, so I decided breakfast with Jerry would be a lot more civilized than sitting around in a noisy bar.

This breakfast, though, was not forthcoming. Jerry was his same old self, smiling and winking at me, making me feel special, then entertaining the guys in the locker room. His "what's the difference between a woman and a sheep?" jokes had gotten to be a running gag, and just when we thought we'd heard them all, he'd come up with a new one — a sheep doesn't light up a cigarette afterwards, a sheep never asks for a fur coat, a sheep doesn't have to fake an orgasm — if she has one, you *know* you're good. He'd always watch me, like these jokes were for my personal amusement, some secret message he was passing my way, but man, if he was hot for what I was hot for, he was sure taking his time. Of course, maybe he was just being careful, like I was. Just when I'd get to the point where I'd decide it was hopeless and I might as well give up on him, he'd come up with some new way to get me all worked up again.

Like his neck exercises. We'd been neglecting our necks, he told me, and it was time to get going. Now my neck, I can honestly say, was the one part of my body I didn't pay attention to. I mean, I never knew anyone to get turned on by a guy's neck. So I glanced over at the neck machine in the corner with a little apprehension; machines you don't use always seem intimidating. It was currently occupied by a mountain of a guy wearing a university football jersey whose head seemed to melt into his shoulders.

''Not the machine,'' Jerry said, following my gaze. ''I got some great buddy exercises.''

''Buddy exercises?''

''Sure, a buddy for my body. Just do what I say.'' He moved in front of me, put both his hands on my forehead, and told me to lean into him as hard as I could; then he repeated the exercise on either side of me, him with his hands on my head, me pushing into him. Then he had me get down on all fours and push up against his hands, which he'd planted on the back of my head. Finally, he told me to stay on my knees, lean my head against his leg, and push. Then we switched and I got to hold his head and have him lean against my leg. I was kind of embarrassed at first, I mean, here we were handling each other, but once I realized no one was paying any attention to us, I started to get into it, feeling the texture of Jerry's hair, pushing my thigh against his face. I looked at the mirror and decided my neck did look a little scrawny and figured these new exercises could easily become the high point of my workouts. After that, whenever I thought about Jerry, I pictured him on his knees, his cheek against my thigh, and I don't have to explain what that led to in my fantasies. So I was convinced once more that he and I were on our way, and that it was just a question of timing.

Once my mood picked up on that front, things seemed to get better down at the store, too. Bud had taken a real liking to me and even started asking for my advice — he told me I had an eye for spotting trends. If Bud didn't have a wife and two kids, I could've gotten interested in him. It was a good thing I had Jerry to keep thoughts like that out of my head. But there was no harm in looking, and sometimes, when Bud was standing close to me, maybe we'd be going through a catalog or looking over invoices, my eyes would wander to the muscles on his forearms or the hair on the back of his neck; I'd started taking an interest in necks. But it never failed, every time Bud and I were in a huddle, I'd feel that darned Judy watching me, smiling in that knowing way of hers. If she made a crack about me licking Bud's ass, I swear I was going to punch her out.

I couldn't make up my mind what she was up to. Why would a lesbian try so hard to be friends with a guy unless it was because she figured he was gay, too? Since no one else in the store went out of his way to be nice to her, I guess she considered us allies. She was always asking me for help on how to ring up this or that sale, make out some refund, stuff she knew perfectly well how to do herself. Then she started sharing her lunch with me, and soon she was packing extra little goodies, cookies, chips, just for me. And all the time she'd be looking and smiling, looking and smiling.

And the things she said. "I'd love to see you in these, Joe," she giggled, holding up a pair of purple Italian racing pants when our first shipment came in. "Just your color."

I tried to stay calm when she pulled things like that, but a couple of times I told her to back off in no uncertain terms. She'd always come up smiling. "You got me my job," she'd say, "so I'm obligated to you. We're soul mates." Or she'd keep telling me how I was *different* from the other guys, nudging me with her arm, saying we had so much in common. Why me? I kept thinking. I didn't want to share secrets with Judy. She must have had dyke friends for all that. For cryin' out loud, that's all women do these days, carry on about how they're sisters and don't need guys. Christ, they even advertise it on their clothes. I see them in the store all the time wearing shirts that say things like "There's only two things wrong with men, what they do and what they say." And here Judy's treating me like one of her girlfriends. When someone's on to you like that, it's hard to say which is worse, to be friendly, which just made the other guys snicker and played into her hand, or keep my distance and risk alienating the very person who had the goods on me. So even though I was scoring high with Bud and doing well at my job, Judy was making me more and more uncomfortable. What's the difference between Judy and a sheep? Help a sheep get a job and it ends up a lamb chop.

SCENE XV

First Impressions

Alec was hardly ever home anymore. He'd been putting in extra time at the record store since the assistant manager had quit, and most nights he went up to campus to watch rehearsals of the play. He came in all excited one time because Kelly, the director, couldn't make up his mind between two ways to stage a number and asked Alec what he thought.

"Just like that!" Alec explained. "He didn't even think about it. Just 'Alec, which do you think works better?' And afterward we talked it over for half an hour, and I suggested a little change and he said next time he'd give it a try. And you know, Joe, I'm sure he's gay. He has to be careful, you know, being a faculty member, and new and all, but he's really very sweet. I caught him looking at me a couple of times, and once he even put his hand on my arm."

When Alec was in a good mood like that, I mean really carried away, which didn't happen very often, he seemed like a different person. His mannerisms would disapear, no more dramatic emphasis on certain words, no more throat clutching and hand waving. I began to suspect that deep down inside, Alec wasn't very happy, that he felt unappreciated and didn't like the way people used him, either for sex or for his ideas. His gestures, I realized, weren't really part of him, more like little bits of theater he used to cover up his feelings. He needed to have something good happen to give him the confidence he lacked, but I was afraid if he didn't assert himself a little more, he'd be limiting his possibilities. So I was glad to see him with a reason to be excited.

Of course he still sang, no matter what kind of mood he was in, but I was used to that, even thought it was kind of funny. Like now, when he was putting the dishes away, singing "He Touched Me." I couldn't tell if he was happy because this Kelly was treating him seriously, or if maybe he was getting hung up on the guy. Whichever it was, I hoped it wouldn't fall through, because I liked seeing him that way.

When Alec was pleased, it showed in the kitchen; he'd try some new recipe or prepare a really elaborate meal. I discovered the records he played or the songs he sang were related to whatever kind of food he was fixing at the time. For instance, when he cooked something Greek, moussaka or dolmades, I'd hear a medley from *Zorba, Illya Darling,* and *The Happiest Girl in the World.* When he made blintzes and borscht, the accompaniment was *Fiddler on the Roof, The Rothschilds,* and *Milk and Honey.* French food meant *Coco, Irma La Douce,* and *Ben Franklin in Paris.* Once I caught on to this, I'd check the album jacket sitting near the stereo and read a few lines of the story as a clue to dinner. That Friday it was *Bravo Giovanni,* with *Carmelina* and *Nine* waiting in the wings, so I knew I was in for an Italian treat. Alec called it "upscale pizza," with smoked salmon, anchovies, and three kinds of cheese. But the Chianti was authentic, and dessert was zabaglione.

"Alec," I asked him right out, "are you in love? Like maybe with that guy Kelly?"

"Pretty transparent, aren't I?"

"Well, I can tell you've been in a good mood lately."

"I'm probably making a fool of myself, but I really

think he likes me. I wish the play would never open, just stay in rehearsal for years and years, with Kelly asking my advice and letting me help with all the details. Does that sound ridiculous?''

''Not really. I know what you mean, how things sometimes seem better in anticipation than when they actually happen. But there's a limit to how long you can hold out. I mean, you could bust a gut just waiting around.''

He raised an eyebrow. ''Who's the lucky guy?''

''What do you mean?''

''Come on, Joe, you've been on a roller coaster yourself, up one day, down the next. You're always in a good mood when you leave for the gym. It's someone there, isn't it?''

''Alec. . . .''

''Oh, come on, Joe. I told you, so level with me.''

''Well, there is this guy. I mean I'm not really sure. . . . In a way I am, but then . . . . Anyhow, it's taking forever.''

''All I know is a few weeks ago we were sitting around complaining about our rotten luck, now we both feel things are looking up. How about we go out on the town tonight? A movie, then we can stop by the Alamo. It's about time I made an appearance on the social scene. Besides, some of the theater people might be there; maybe I'll hear something about Kelly.''

There was a time I'd have thought twice about going to the bar with Alec, but things were different now. *He* was different. Or at least I thought so. Or maybe I'd just gotten used to him. In any case, the fact that we lived together was no secret, everyone in the bar knew that. So this time I let him pick the movie, and we hit the Alamo around ten. It was still early, and I was curious to see if Jerry might turn up, but I never saw him.

Alec and I sat in a corner with our beers. By 11 there

was a pretty good crowd, and I'd been there often enough that now I recognized some faces. Alec knew just about everyone, or at least knew who they all were, and he told me lots of funny stories. There was one guy he pointed out who everyone called Capt. Hook because of the way his cock bent, another with a dimple in his chin that Alec swore was matched by a dimple on the tip of his dick. And a big fellow, standing alone, he warned me about — he used his teeth, and if you weren't careful, you ended up black and blue in places no one wanted to be black and blue. His nickname was Jaws. I got a good laugh from all this, but I couldn't help thinking, no wonder everyone knew how big Alec was, these poor guys had no secrets. And I understood why Tony'd had the good sense to insist we not mix with people like them.

Of course the Birdies showed up and went to hang out in the back with other swishy types. But Alec stayed with me and I was glad not to be left alone. The bar was packed, but I wondered if anyone ever got down to serious cruising. Everybody seemed afraid to break away from his little group of friends. Guys would look around while someone else was talking or peer over the head of whoever they were with, but except for a few quick glances, no one seemed to have the nerve to try and make contact. A lot of guys stopped to talk to Alec or just say hello, and some of them weren't bad. And more than a couple, I must say, gave me the once-over. But if Alec introduced us, they'd just nod or smile and make their way through the crowd to where their friends were waiting.

"Alec, doesn't anybody come here to cruise?"

He shrugged. "Everyone knows everyone, so there's no hurry. If someone new came in, they'd give him a thorough going-over, discuss his hair, his clothes, his manner, probably put him down. But they'd all be wonderng how they were going to meet him without running the risk of everyone seeing them get shot down. Then at closing time, if the poor guy lasted that long, they'd crowd around the bar for one last drink, everyone trying to catch his eye, then follow him out onto the street, away from the audience. That's how it is in this town."

No wonder I hadn't had any luck. I realized that all those times I'd felt people were talking about me, they undoubtedly were. And I'd never made it to closing time.

"Why" Alec asked, "is there someone you want to meet?"

"No, I was just asking." Actually there was one guy I'd found myself watching, just to have someone to look at. He was tall, a little taller than me, so he was hard to miss, with sandy hair and great cheekbones. From what I could see, he had a good build. At least when he brought his drink up to his mouth there was a noticeable bulge in his bicep. Young guys don't think much about staying shape — they don't have to. And among the gays, thin was in. So when I spotted this guy with some muscle on him, I couldn't take my eyes off him. But there was something about him that struck me as a little. . .wrong. For starters, he was standing in the back with Tom and Randy and their crowd. He hung around the edge of the group, like maybe he just wanted to be standing near people he knew, only half-listening to what they were saying. He had an almost-smile on his face that never changed, and he wasn't talking much, which was in his favor, at least as far as that bunch went. But there was something else about him. Even though he was just standing there, shifting his weight from foot to foot, he stood out. Maybe it was the long scarf hanging around his neck or the way he flicked his hair back, a certain arrogance. I just couldn't make up my mind.

"Alec, I, uh, suppose you'd really rather be back there with your friends. We don't have to stay here." If he joined them, I could shuffle around nearby, get a better look at this guy, see if Alec knew him.

"I came with you, and I know you don't want to hang out with them."

"Whatever." I didn't want to push it or he'd know I had some other motive. Or worse yet, one of the Birdies would notice my staring and then I'd be in for it. After a few minutes I saw that creep Andy come in. He looked over at me and Alec and smirked before he turned to his friends. I felt they were all sneaking glances over at us, and I could have sworn I heard someone say Tony's name. Maybe I was getting paranoid. I mean, why should a bunch of turkeys like that bother me? But when Alec said he was ready to leave, I didn't argue. I managed a last look over at the tall guy, and our eyes met. Neither of us looked away for a few seconds, till he flicked his hair back and threw the scarf over his shoulder with a flourish, and I thought, he's no different from the others, and we left.

SCENE XVI

Merrily We Roll Along

By this time it was the middle of March, and if anyone had told me back in January that I'd end up like this, I wouldn't have believed it. Nothing was working out the way it was supposed to. Tony, for instance. I sure had him figured wrong. I always assumed he felt about me the way I did about him and that he wouldn't let me get away. But he did. Sure, I still thought about him and missed him, but I was beginning to realize it wasn't so much him I missed as having someone around, not needing to worry about where or when or with whom I'd make it. And I sure wasn't making it now. Tony didn't even enter into my fantasies any more, at least not all the time. Needless to say Jerry had the starring role, a buddy for my body. In my fantasies we'd do it the way I like it, not the way Tony always wanted it. I love sex. I love it long, slow, and all over. Tony liked it short, fast, and to the point. ''Use it or lose it,'' he'd say, tugging at my belt.

The funny thing was, the sex got better as our relationship went downhill. In the beginning, we argued about it. He'd humor me for a while, but he always got his way in the end — which is just where he wanted it. But as the months went by, Tony cooled down; it took him longer and longer to get in the mood. Which was OK, since that let me take the time to explore all those secret places I lusted after — the little patch of fuzz in the small of his back, the hollow under his Adam's apple. I finally felt we were making love instead of orgasms, and that that was how a relationship should be after the initial passion dies down. If it happened less often, it was worth waiting for. But then I found out what he was really up to, and I realized he was just plain worn out. He'd used it *and* lost it! And I was never really satisfied.

I guess what I missed about Tony was the way he talked to me, told me we were meant for each other, a special pair, all that stuff about staying exclusive. He made me swear I'd never make it with anyone else, and I never did, for the whole year we were together. When I asked him to swear the same thing, he'd accuse me of not trusting him. If I asked didn't he trust me, he'd tell me it was because I was so hot and handsome that he worried about me, and I'd end up eating out of his hand. I never did get him to swear to me. I've always been a good judge of people, but maybe I didn't know Tony like I thought I did.

Then there was Alec. I hadn't expected to stay in that apartment for more than a few days, just like I never planned to let him cook for me. But I looked forward to diner time, and I'd long since decided it would be easier to find a place in the summer, when all the students cleared out I'd even gotten used to his friends, at least to their always being around. And when I let it slip out down at the store that I knew Harold Waldman, people were goddam *impressed.* "No kidding," Bud told me. "He's my favorite part of the news."

"Going show biz on us?" Judy asked with a smirk. "Why don't you bring him down and introduce us all?" I knew what she was thinking, one more way she had me pegged. I just mumbled that I didn't know him all that well. Just what I'd need, Harold down at the store trying on Italian seamless racing pants over his cock ring.

At least there was one bright spot in all this —

meeting Jerry. I'd made up my mind to set a date for our get-together on my way to the gym one morning. But he looked real bad that day; I could tell he didn't feel well. "Joe, my man, gotta pack it in early. I think I have a touch of the flu."

And just when I'd started getting off on his buddy exercises. After a few days, I thought about getting his address from the club owner, figured I'd pay a visit and cheer him up. But I chickened out. Without the weight lifting I was afraid we wouldn't have much to say to each other, and he sure wouldn't be in the mood for that special talk I had planned if he was sick. So I let the lifting slide and drifted back to the machines. But I'd forgotten what weight I did on which machines, and what with my neck already sore from pressing so hard against Jerry's leg, I strained a muscle on the overhead pull-down and was sidelined myself for a couple of days.

No, things were not working out the way I'd imagined on that cold day in January. But spring was a week away, and the flowers pictured on the calendar reminded me of the sampler that hung over grandma's sofa: "No day is so long that night won't fall, Nor night so black the sun won't call." You just have to take it one day at a time. And that's what I tried to tell Alec, who was having more black days than sunny ones. I figured it had to do with that guy Kelly.

"He said he'd come over sometime to look through my albums," Alec said, when I asked if he was making any progress. "But he's so busy. The show's a few weeks away; we're never really alone together. What about your friend, the one from the gym?"

"He's got the flu."

"Tough luck."

"'Yeah."

"Joe?"

"Mhm?"

"I think I'm gonna get canned."

"From the store?"

"I think so. I've had this feeling, the last couple of weeks, they've been watching me. Once in the manager's office I saw a piece of paper with my name on it. He snatched it up before I could see what it was. It looked like a file or report. And the owner was in, and the two of them were just standing there, looking at me."

"Has anyone said anything?"

"Not yet. All I can think is it must've been because of a customer I had a big fight with. This idiot comes in with a pile of used records and tells me they're rare. But they were reissues, every one of them. He's waving around this copy of *I Can Get It for You Wholesale* and telling me it's worth fifteen or twenty bucks, and I'm trying to show him how you can tell from the label it's a reissue, pulling out catalogs, showing him numbers, and we go through this with every record — *Top Banana, Greenwillow.* He accused me of trying to cheat him, made a big scene. I wasn't as polite as I could have been. I guess he complained."

"If no one's said anything, don't worry about it."

"Easy for you to say. What'll I do if they can me?"

"Alec, you don't know that they are. Besides, it's not the end of the world. There are other jobs."

"Yeah, like what? It may be a dead end, but it pays the rent. What would you do if you lost your job?"

"I don't know. Go back to school, I guess."

"That's what they all say."

"Don't you believe me?"

"Why don't you go back now? You plan to sell sweat socks all your life?"

"I'll go back. Maybe next year."

"Sure. Will they let you?"

"Why shouldn't they?"

"You flunked out, didn't you?"

"Who said I flunked out?" I was getting mad now. Just like Alec, always turning the conversation around to me.

"Well, did you or didn't you?"

"I quit. Who told you I flunked out?"

"Don't get so worked up. I thought you left school because you had to."

"And I want to know why you thought that."

"It's just what . . .people said."

"What people? Dammit, Alec, tell me."

"Look, one day you're in school and the next day you're running around with Tony showing off to all the world and then you're moving in with him and you're not in school. So everyone *down at the bar* assumed you flunked out."

"Why was everyone so interested in me? I never knew any of those people."

"Joe, Tony was well-known. So when he started parading around town with you in tow, people were curious."

"Tony, well-known? He wasn't friendly with those guys. They weren't his type. Whatever they made up about us, it was just because they were jealous."

"Believe what you want."

"Meaning?"

"What do you want me to tell you? That Tony didn't know a soul? That he dropped out of the sky one day with you on his arm?"

"Did you know Tony?"

"If you must know, I did. And so did a lot of other people. You don't want to believe me, fine. I'm depressed enough without all this. I was hoping for sympathy, not a shouting match."

I was sorry I'd argued with him, what with the mood he was in, but he was like that, sometimes, repeating gossip that his flitty little friends made up. Like me flunking out. True, my grades started to slip after I met Tony, but it wasn't really my fault. He got impatient whenever I hit the books. He'd wait till I was studying for an exam or writing a paper, then decide to try on some sexy new clothes or lie on the bed and make a big show of rearranging his crotch every few minutes, whatever it took to get my attention. "I'm doing OK without ever finishing college," he'd say. "Wouldn't you rather spend the time with me?" So I decided to quit. Just before I'd have flunked out.

But what did those barflies know about that? They never heard it from Tony, they just jumped to their own conclusions. Made-up lies. Sour grapes because they envied us, like Tony said. It's a good thing we stayed exclusive. I liked Alec, but there were certain things we couldn't talk about without ending up in an argument.

Still, I felt sorry for him, and not just because he was worried about his job. He was also afraid that once that show was over, he wouldn't see Kelly anymore. He'd walk around the apartment singing these real downers: "My Man's Gone Now," "Lonely Town," "Never Will I Marry." I suppose his suffering was real, but it was somewhat undercut by a wicked rendition of Katharine Hepburn on "Always Mademoiselle." One thing was sure, he wasn't in the mood to forgive me for having argued with him. He announced that he was having friends over in a few days to watch the Academy Awards and made a point of telling me to plan on being out that night, since his guest list didn't include the kind of people I'd want to be around.

So the night of the party I grabbed a hamburger after the store closed, then stopped in at the Alamo. The set there was tuned to the Oscars, too, and the few people in the place were glued to the screen. I stuck it out for a while, but finally had no choice but to go home. I could hear the shrieks and shouts as I headed up the stairs. Tom and Randy were there, and Harold, "Oh, my Godding" every few minutes because he'd predicted the winners on his TV spot the week before, and the sportscaster, who you could tell thought Harold was a flake, was sure to razz him the next night for any he'd missed. Hardly the crowd I liked coming home to, but I could handle them well enough by ignoring them.

Then I noticed someone else, someone who'd never been over before, fair-haired and high-cheeked and well built — the guy I'd seen in the bar with Alec. He watched me hang up my coat, I was sure of it, so instead of ducking into my room, I went into the kitchen. I got a glass of juice and leaned in the doorway.

"Oh, God," Harold was moaning, "the sympathy vote won out. I should have known! Why didn't I pick her? And would you *look* at that dress. At her age. My housekeeper wouldn't dust the floor with it. And do you know who does her gowns? It must have cost her a fortune."

I stood there a while, one eye on the screen, one on that guy. He was wearng a French CPO jacket, in blue, like I'd seen in some catalog, over what I thought I recognized as Danish parachute pants, in gray, with a drawstring in the back. Loose clothes weren't my taste. I work hard on my body and like clothes that show it off, but on him, with his long legs stretched out, it all looked good, as good as Jerry looked in his workout pants. Jerry was still sick, and I guess I needed someone to focus my attention on till he got back. So why not Mr. Cheekbones, here? At least I knew he was gay. With Jerry it was one step backward for every two forward. In the meantime, there was no harm in looking.

"So who's won what?" I asked during a commercial.

"Nothing important," Alec said coldly. He was still upset with me and probably thought I'd come back to make fun of his friends. "You just saw the supporting actress award; the rest have been for technical stuff."

"There's room here on the sofa next to me, beautiful," Harold said, patting the cushion. "I'm having a *terrible* night and if I miss my predictions, I'll need *something* to hold on to."

The good-looking guy was sitting on the other end of the sofa and glanced over at me with the almost-smile he'd had that first night I saw him. Maybe he thought Harold was as ridiculous as I did. Or maybe he'd heard all that bar gossip and was laughing at me. Well I'd show him. I'd have a seat right there next to him, whether he liked it or not. Before I could move, Randy jumped up from the big pillow he'd been perched on and took the place on the sofa.

"Grab me, Harold, and I'll scratch your contacts out."

Harold looked at me and shrugged. "I lose again, huh, big fella?" The good-looking guy kind of smiled but kind of tried not to.

"I don't think Joe is really interested in this, are you Joe?" Alec didn't want me around and clearly had no intention of introducing me to that guy. I gave up and went to my room.

But after a while I got bored and decided that those twerps, including the big guy with the smug look on his face, weren't going to force me to hide in there, and I found lots of reasons to go out into the living room. I was sure that guy was watching me. Once he was coming out of the kitchen just as I came out of the bathroom and he sort of nodded. Maybe he hadn't been laughing at me. There was still something about him. He moved slowly, gracefully, I hated to admit it, not too butch. What the hell, did I expect anything else from that bunch? I was better off concentrating on a real man, like Jerry. If only he'd get over that flu.

"Who was the guy in the gray pants?" I asked Alec after they'd gone.

"What do you care? He's a friend of Tom and Randy's."

"Just asking. Is he your friend, too?"

"Interested?"

"I've never seen the guy before." At least not close up.

"His name is Rob and he's a dancer and he's working on a master's degree in performing arts, so he's no one you'd want to know."

"Alec, I'm sorry I argued with you the other night. I'm sorry your show is coming up in a couple of weeks and you're not making any progress with that guy you like, and I'm sorry your'e worried about your job. But I was upset, too. How do you think I feel when I hear that the whole town gossips about me?"

"I try not to tell you those things, but you always press me. Besides, I just assumed you knew."

"Are we friends again?"

"Were we ever? Sorry, I don't want to start another fight. Friends."

The next night he made a peace offering, a multicourse Oriental banquet accompanied by his favorite numbers from *Flower Drum Song, The King and I,* and *Pacific Overtures.* We watched Harold on the TV, trying to grin through the sportscaster's jibes, and we both laughed when he blurted out that he'd give his right arm for the lamé scarf the best actress winner had on.

When I got into bed that night, I was feeling a lot better for having patched things up with Alec. But for some reason, I couldn't get my mind off that friend of his, Rob. OK, so he was good-looking and he had a great build. But he was a theater type and hung out with all those people I couldn't stand and had a funny way of flicking back his hair. I'd be much better off with Jerry. I resolved that if Jer wasn't back at the gym within a couple of days, I'd find out where he lived, go see him, and press him for a definite date — at the Alamo, for that breakfast he was always promising, or any place else he named. It was time to get the ball rolling. I mean, things were really bad when even Alec's friends started looking good.

SCENE XVII

Pins and Needles

I never did get around to visiting Jerry. I figured if it was me, I wouldn't want anyone to see me sick — hair greasy, skin pale, maybe one eye on the john door in case I had to make a run for it. I didn't want to put Jerry in that position. When he finally showed up at the gym, he was still kind of washed out. I could tell he'd really been sick.

"No heavy lifting, Joe, my man, gotta get my strength back up." He did some easy curls and flies, then moved to the machines, so we didn't get much chance to talk. But the next time I saw him he was feeling a lot better.

"So, uh, Jer, when are we going to have that breakfast?"

"Real soon, Joe. That bug I had set me back at work, so I'll need a little time. But you and I are gonna get together and have a good talk. Not with all these dudes around, you know, with their dumb jokes."

"Maybe next week? Say, Wednesday?" I'd followed him into the locker room even though I wasn't quite finished with my workout. He thought for a minute.

"No good. Business meeting. But real soon, Joe. You and me. I've got something to discuss with you that's gonna make you awfully glad you met me." He grabbed my shoulder and gave it a squeeze.

It wasn't much, but it was all I had to look forward

to. And enough to make me so cheerful around the apartment I even caught myself humming "Our Private World" from one of Alec's favorite shows.

"I'm glad someone has something to sing about," he muttered. Even though he was thick with Kelly, now he complained that the director was taking him for granted. " 'Alec, could you help out with this? Could you look for that? Would you find the place in the script?' At least he could thank me when he steals my ideas."

That's about all you could expect from these theatrical types, I thought to myself. They were all in it to satisfy their own egos. Tom and Randy were always bitching about someone upstaging them or blocking their light. And Harold, he was nothing *but* ego. Sure, he made jokes about himself, but that was just as self-serving as everything else he did. So in a way I felt Alec had gotten himself into this mess by hanging around with those jerks just to get in good with some director who he wasn't even sure really liked him. Unlike me, Alec was not a good judge of character.

On top of all that, he was still convinced he was going to be fired. The store manager had called in one of the other clerks and asked what he thought of Alec's work. The guy liked Alec, told the boss he was smart, but what about the other employees? He was afraid they'd all been interviewed, too, and he didn't know where he stood with them.

"It's all I can do to get through each day. I feel like everyone's spying on me."

"Why don't you just go in and ask the boss what's up?"

"And then what? Have him tell me they're not happy with me and let me go right there? At least I'm getting paid while the inquisition is going on."

"Well I still think you're jumping to conclusions."

"You know what really scares me? We've been short

in the cash register a few times lately. A couple of bucks here, a couple there. One night it was $45. What if they think I took it? If they accuse me, I'll die. I can't take it much longer, everyone watching me.''

I told him he was imagining it all, but how did I know what was coming down? I didn't enjoy seeing him like that, but my mood was so good I didn't want to let him get to me. That Friday, at the gym, Jerry finally came through. I was doing the lateral raise, the first exercise on the double shoulder machine, when he came over.

''Monday morning, Joe, how about it? We'll work out at the regular time then go over to Peabody's for one of those big breakfast specials. Plenty of time for that little talk we've had in mind. Is it a go?''

''Great, Jer, Monday morning.'' I was so excited I forgot to lower the weight for the second exercise, the overhead press, and almost threw my shoulder out.

Despite the pain, I was walking on air for the the rest of the day. ''What's got you so happy, muscle man?'' Judy asked me. ''You've been on a high all week.''

''Things are OK, that's all.''

''It's good seeing you like this. Cheers up the whole place. You're a pretty moody guy, you know?''

''Me? I have my good days and my bad days, like everyone else.''

''No, not like everyone else. I mean, when you're depressed, you're DEPRESSED. Some days I don't even want to talk to you.''

''I hadn't noticed.'' I should be so lucky.

''Take my word for it. It's OK, though. A man should let his emotions out. You know, not be afraid to show his feminine side.''

''Who are you calling feminine?''

And I'll be damned if she didn't start laughing. ''Joe, you're terrific. And I'll tell you something else.'' I didn't say anything, so after a while she went on. "I've got a little surprise for you."

"I hate surprises." I was afraid this was it — the big confession. I looked around to see if there was any way to escape, maybe a customer to help. Maybe a hole in the floor I could fall through.

"This isn't the time to go into details, but believe me, you're in for it. We're so much alike, you and I. You'll see."

What did she want from me? Face it, gay men and women don't really have that much in common. You only had to compare Judy and me to see that. I at least care about how I look. But Judy didn't wear any makeup, cut her hair like she'd put a bowl over her head. Never wore anything with style. For all I knew, she was one of those radical types who never shaved their legs. I shuddered to think what was going on in their armpits. And overweight girls can *do* something, take care of themselves, dress in ways that make them look more or less OK. But some gay women I've seen just don't try. Not like the guys. Slim, good haircuts, trendy clothes. So I didn't know why Judy was so hot on us being friends. OK, I'll admit the other guys in the store weren't always nice to her. That must have been tough, and I sometimes felt sorry for her. But that was no reason for her not to go on a diet. I mean, she could be thin and still be a volleyball coach, couldn't she?

Later that afternoon I was in the back room trying to figure out an imaginative way to display knee pads when I heard some kind of commotion out front, breathy whispers like someone was upset. I heard Judy's voice, too. Then she came back to find me — I had a visitor, she said. I went out front and there was Alec, pale as death, one hand clutching his heart, leaning on the counter with the other. Just what I'd always dreaded, him or one of his friends coming in and making a scene. I didn't really think it could happen. After all, what would the Birdies want in a sporting goods store?

Their idea of exercise was turning a record over. So why was Alec here, gaunt and breathless, looking like the world was about to end?

"Alec, what is it? What are you doing here?"

"Joe, I had to talk to someone. What am I going to do? I'll *die!*"

It seemed to me he was at his absolute worst, and I was on the brink of humiliation. "What's the matter?" I whispered. "Calm down. Control yourself." I noticed Judy was still there, watching all this, and I felt like dying myself. What if Bud or Ralph or one of the other guys came along and saw this gawky queen doing a Joan Crawford routine right there in front of the Heavy Hands display? I grabbed his arm and led him to the shoe department where he could sit down. "Now what's so awful that you had to come running over here?"

"This is it. They're going to fire me today."

"How do you know?"

"The boss just left for lunch. He told me he wanted to see me the *minute* he got back. Said it was important. Said I should get Bernie to cover my department. Maybe for the whole afternoon. Now you tell me — why would they need someone to cover my department if they weren't going to can me?"

I had to admit it didn't sound good. I was afraid he was going to start crying right there in the shoe department just when a couple of college guys started looking over some new models.

"Alec, it'll be all right. Whatever happens, don't worry."

"How will I find another job? How will I live? Pay the rent? Buy the groceries?"

"Everything will be fine. I've got a job. I'm not going to throw you out of your own apartment. I'll help you out."

''You will?''

''Of course. Now please, calm down. Pull yourself together. You're too good for that cruddy job, anyway. You've said it yourself. So take it like a man.''

''I will, Joe. I promise.'' He stood up and and shook his head, like he was coming up for air. The two college guys were looking around impatiently, waiting to be helped, and I didn't want to miss the sale. Or miss getting a better look at them, since they were both hot numbers.

''I gotta go, Alec. Now remember, be a man.''

''Like Florence of Arabia?'' He saw me wince. ''Sorry. It's from a song.'' He tried to smile.

I smiled back. ''Yeah, like Florence of Arabia.'' I remembered having heard the line; I think Chita Rivera did the number, in the show.

SCENE XVIII

On the Town

After I'd finished with those two guys, Judy came over to me again. "That was real sweet, Joe, the way you helped out your buddy."

"He's not my buddy. He's just . . .someone I know. He was passing by and needed to talk to someone."

"Passing by? From the record store across the way?"

"You know him?"

"Just seen him there. Don't be defensive. You don't have to apologize for your friends. No big deal. This is me, Judy, remember? I understand."

"There's nothing to understand. I told you, he's just someone I know."

"Joe, I've always said that tough exterior isn't the real you. This just proves it. Here you are, this big muscular hunk, there's your friend, skinny and vulnerable looking, coming to you for help. It's like I always say, you're a sensitive guy. I feel I'm getting to know you better and better."

"Anything you say, Judy." And I walked away.

Alec's visit happened around one-thirty, and when I hadn't heard from him after an hour or two I managed to put it out of my mind. We got really busy in the store and I spent a lot of time with this hot black hunk who was interested in a set of weights. I tried to persuade him to join the gym — I wouldn't mind sharing the sauna with *him*.

I must have done too good a job; he left without buying anything.

Thinking about being naked in the sauna made me think of Jerry and our meeting Monday morning. So during my break, when I'd sort of been planning to go over and see Alec, or at least give him a call, I started daydreaming instead about Jerry, imagining our conversation and what would come after it. I did something I'd never done before, snuck into the staff john and gave myself a quickie. When I came out, Judy was standing at the door, smiling.

Bud was in a rotten mood at closing time; a big delivery arrived late, and he wanted it unloaded before he'd let us leave. So I didn't get home till around seven. On my way up the stairs I remembered about Alec and figured I'd better brace myself for the worst. I wasn't in the mood to see him through a crying jag and had no idea what I could say to make him feel better.

I was more than a little surprised to hear him singing happily in his room. " 'You think of me as superfluous, he thinks of me as superlative.' " I called to him. He came out all dressed up and grinning.

"You OK, Alec?"

He did a little pirouette. "Joe, you are looking at the new assistant manager of the Wax Works. Not just the soundtrack and original cast department, but the whole ever-mother-loving store." The full story came gushing out, how they'd had their eye on him all those weeks because they were planning to promote him, how impressed they were when he'd sorted out the records and made a collector's bin of rare shows that he sold for fifteen, twenty bucks, sometimes more, and how people from the city even drove out because they'd heard he knew his stuff. "They spoke to everyone in the whole store — hardly anyone had anything bad to say about me. They *like* me down there. Can you believe that?"

I was surprised. Not that I didn't think Alec was smart or know his way around those records, but because he was, well, so. . .obvious. I'd've thought they knew all about him, put up with him, maybe even made fun of him. But I guess not. That's something I'd noticed when I went out with him, to the movies or for a snack. Other people seemed to think he was OK, even when I was cringing at some outrageous thing he'd say or some gesture he'd make. I guess I'm just more perceptive than most people. It's always been one of my strong points.

Alec insisted we go out to dinner, someplace nice, so I went in for a quick shower. He was singing his head off "Will everyone here kindly step to the rear and let a winner lead the way?" I kind of got into the rhythm while I lathered myself up; I was in a good mood, too, and was looking forward to going out. I was in a hurry, I suppose, because I forgot myself and, carried away by his song, left the bathroom door open, something I was usually careful not to do. I almost slipped on the tile floor when Alec let out a shriek.

"What's wrong?" I shouted, grabbing on to the sink.

"Wrong? Wrong? On the contrary, my dear boy. I have just glimpsed the perfect ass. Did you know you have a perfect ass?"

"Alec, for crying out loud. I almost killed myself." I closed the door and pulled my pants on.

"But really, Joe," he said when I came out, "you don't see an ass like that often. There's no line."

"What are you talking about?"

"No fold, under your buns. Like one big muscle from your tush down your legs. No under-the-cheek crease. A beauteous maximus."

I was all set to give him a good talking to. This kind of stuff was out of bounds. But he was discussing it so — good-naturedly — I couldn't really get mad. Besides, I knew my ass was one of my especially good features, and I was secretly pleased that he appreciated it. As long as he didn't get any ideas . . . .

He insisted we go to the fanciest place in town, and it wasn't till we were there that it even dawned on me that this was where Tony had worked. I'd been thinking so much about Jerry that I'd almost managed to put Tony out of my mind. Still, I felt a little twinge when we went into the lounge to wait for our table. The bartender was a real hunk, Greek athlete type, the buttons of his vest straining over his chest, lots of curly dark hair like a stain under his white shirt. I'd seen him once or twice when I was waiting for Tony to get off. Imagine my surprise when he greets Alec like a long-lost friend.

''Hey, Alec, how ya doing? Haven't seen you around.''

''Hi, Nick. I haven't been going out much. This is Joe.''

He put out his hand. ''Say, don't I know you? Sure, Tony! That's it, you were Tony's live-in.'' I was having trouble keeping up with all this. How come everybody always knew everybody else except me? I mumbled a hello. ''What do you hear from old Tony? I understand he's doing good. Real good.''

''Oh?''

''Yeah, I got these friends in the city, they work out at his gym. He's got this modeling job or something. Or was it movies?''

''I wouldn't know.''

He shook his head. ''That Tony, he was really something, wasn't he? What a guy!''

I didn't know exactly what he meant, but something about the way he said it made a little red light go on in my head. I began to think of all those nights Tony was late, especially the times he said he had to help with bar inventory. How often did they have to count the glasses?

''Sorry about that,'' Alec whispered when they called us for a table. ''Do you want to go somewhere else?''

"No, no, it's OK. You really do know everyone, don't you?"

During our dinner, Alec told me all about Nick and how he and some professor from the university had this thing going, drove into the city once a week, took a room in a hotel and screwed all day. Then they'd come back to town and go their separate ways. "It's been going on for years," he said.

"Alec, how do you know all this?"

He shrugged. "It's common knowledge. I just hear things."

"Yeah, I know, it's a small town. How did they meet?" I was interested in learning how guys got together. It seemed impossible to me.

"Baldwin Hall basement, the hottest spot on campus, a great big men's room in that building on the quad. Eight stalls in a row and a dozen urinals arranged in a horseshoe. Plus a janitor's closet you could lock from the inside. At lunchtime, guys would be lined up down the hall."

I hated to think I'd been missing out on something like that. "What happened?"

"Some secretary got curious when she saw fourteen guys go in and no one come out for over an hour. Called the campus cops and the place was busted."

"So what's it like now?"

"They converted it into an office. But the marble walls are still there and in the winter, when the windows are closed, you can get a whiff of that old john. Many a freshman got an education down there."

"Including you?"

"Are you kidding? I taught a few professors a thing or two."

We both laughed. But I couldn't help thinking, that must've been the golden age.

SCENE XIX

I Had a Ball

We ended our celebration with a couple of brandies. What with the drinks we had in the bar, the bottle of wine with our meal, and the after-dinner drinks, I had a little buzz going. It seemed a shame to go home, so we headed over to the Alamo. It was still early, and we nursed a couple of beers while we watched the crowd change from college kids to gays. Alec told me that the original owner had tried to keep the gays out, so they organized a campus-wide boycott, the start of gay activism at the school. The new owners were cool, but everyone knew that if you were straight you didn't hang around after eleven. I tried to remember if Jerry had dropped any hints about the time he'd been there and kept an eye on the door just in case.

By 11:15 the crowd was pretty good. I recognized quite a few guys and knew the patterns that formed. The preppy college crowd stayed to themselves in a corner, and a group of older men from the town hung out at the end of the bar, watching the college kids in the mirror. The theater crowd, Alec's friends, always stood in the back, where there had once been a pool table. But, Alec explained, pool tables attract dykes, and after a fist fight once broke out between them and a couple of transvestites who came over from the city, the pool table had to go. An image crossed my mind of Judy hauling off at some six-foot drag queen. My money was on Judy — the follow-through of a volleyball serve could bust someone's jaw. Worse yet, another image came to me — meeting Judy at the bar. I was relieved when Alec told me the gay women had their own hangout down on the county road. At least I was safe from Judy at the Alamo.

"This place really jumps in September," he told me, "when the school year starts. The old-timers turn out to look over the newcomers. By the middle of the semester, the new guys have been assimilated, everyone's had whoever he's going to have and it's back to this again. It happens all over in June when summer school starts."

"Sounds pretty bleak to me."

"The bar isn't where the action is. Most of the good stuff happens at the parties."

"What parties?"

"When the bar closes. Someone throws a party almost every week. Didn't Tony ever take you to one?"

"No, I never heard about them." Hmm, more of Tony's late nights?

"People mingle more. It's easier to score. Hold on a minute." He climbed off his stool and disappeared in the back. After a couple of minutes he retured with the location of that night's party.

"Want to go?"

"I'm not sure, Alec. I don't know anyone, I wouldn't feel like I really belong."

"You won't meet anyone if you don't mix. Besides, it's OK if you go with me. Rob said it's an open house."

"Rob?"

"You met Rob. The dancer. At our place the night of the Oscars."

How could I forget Rob and his cheekbones? Only I hadn't met him. Not yet. "Well, maybe we can go for a little while. If you don't mind."

He shrugged. "What's one party more or less? But it won't get started till the Alamo closes."

We nursed a couple more beers and watched the clock until last call. The bar emptied quickly and everyone drifted down the hill to the part of town that the students lived in. The apartment where the party was being held didn't look big enough to hold half the people who'd been in the bar. It was typical of the dumps in that neighborhood, cracked ceilings and dirty walls, just the kind of student dive I was afraid I might have ended up in if I hadn't stumbled onto Alec. Most of the crowd from the Alamo was there, plus others who'd heard about the goings-on. It looked like anyone who wanted to could go, and I didn't feel so out of it, as long as I stayed close to Alec. People just dumped their coats in a corner and it didn't take long for the place to fill up with smoke. I'd already had a lot to drink but I took a glass of cheap jug wine when I could, just to have something to hold. I followed Alec through the mob till he found the Birdies and other friends from their play. I didn't intend to talk to any of them, but I was at least glad there was a group I could sort of be part of. Rob wasn't anywhere at this end of the room, so I kept looking around till finally I saw his head towering over the crowd in the kitchen. I made my way in his direction to get a better look. He had on an Algerian campaign shirt under a Canadian bombadier jacket and what I guessed were Nairobi field pants, khaki. He looked sexy and elegant and bored, which, considering the company, I took to be a good sign.

After a while some of the crowd moved down the hall to another apartment where there was a stereo and dancing. Someone opened the windows to clear the air, but I was feeling pretty dizzy. There were a number of great-looking guys at that party, and I must say quite a few looked me over pretty good and nodded or even smiled, but I was getting the feeling this was going to be like the bar — you'd have to hang around till the end before anyone got anywhere. Then I caught sight of that guy Andy with a bunch of his friends, so I turned and made my way back to where Alec was. His group was making a big fuss over his promotion, and when I heard Randy say that his "big sister" was making good, I decided to have a walk around and see if I could get a better look at Rob and his fancy clothes and the heck with anyone who didn't like it. I got that way, when I'd been drinking.

I hadn't planned to finish the glass of wine I was holding, let alone have any more, but when you're trying to act like you're having a good time you have to do something, so I gulped the last swallow and went looking for a bottle. Besides, I didn't see Rob in the kitchen anymore, and looking for a drink was a good way to find out where he'd gone. Of course, compared to someone like Jerry, Rob was too flamboyant for me, and I certainly wasn't interested in any friend of the Birdies, especially some dancer. I just liked looking at him, like you admire a cat when it sits in one of those typical cat poses. He was like a cat in that respect, a big beautiful tiger, with an air about him, as if *he* was always posing. But he'd shift his weight or move his arm and naturally fall into another graceful stance. I even liked to watch him walk. Sometimes, at the gym, I thumbed through dance magazines. Not that I was turned on by tights, but dancers have the best bodies, better than most athletes. And I noticed this funny thing — I'd never seen an ugly dancer. They always looked great. Proud, aristocratic. Just like Rob.

By that time, with all I'd drunk plus the heavy smell of pot wafting through the air, it was all I could do to stagger around the room. There weren't as many people now, and I was able to get my hands on some wine and make my way back to where Alec was. At least, where I thought he was, since he wasn't there now. I had an instant of panic at the thought that he might have gone and left me there, but I finally saw him and tottered over to where his group had relocated. He was sitting on the arm of a chair occupied by someone I didn't know. And next to him, on the sofa, was Rob, like a king on his throne. He looked up at me as I approached, and just as I was about to say hi, Randy sat down right on his lap and Tom plopped himself onto the sofa beside him, and the two of them started pawing at him in a way that I thought was totally disgusting. He sat there with that almost-smile on his face, like they were just a minor nuisance, gnats not worth waving away. Alec was talking to him now, telling him something about that show they were doing. Rob just nodded and smiled, nodded and smiled, while the Birdies caressed each other and him at the same time, a scene that really turned me off. And to think I'd wanted to say hello. I decided it might be about time to go to bed. The next morning I'd be a day closer to breakfast with Jerry, a real man who appreciated another real man when he saw one. I downed the rest of my wine and grabbed Alec's shoulder. "Alec, I think. . . ." Except I couldn't quite say *what* I thought.

He took my arm. "Whoa, steady. I think we'd better get you home."

"But Alec. . . ."

"But nothing." He had his arm around me and was leading me to the door. Someone gave us our coats and I somehow managed to get mine on, but it wasn't till we were outside in the cold air that I started coming around. The walk home helped clear my head, and I was feeling a little better when we got inside. Alec made some coffee and settled me onto the sofa with a mugful.

"Looks like someone who can't hold his liquor had a little more than he should have tonight," he said.

"I'm OK."

"I'll bet. Where does it hurt?"

"My head feels like it's floating about two feet over my body."

He stood behind me and started to rub the back of my neck. "This'll make you feel better." Then he started to massage my shoulders.

"That feels good."

He came around in front of me and took my coffee mug out of my hand. "Lie down on your stomach and I'll give you one of Alec's specials." I stretched out and he started to knead my muscles. It really did feel good. He seemed to be getting into it, too.

"You like my ass, Alec?"

"Yeah. I told you, a great ass." He moved his hands down and began rubbing my behind and thighs. I was floating, feeling better and better.

"You wanna see my ass?"

He took his hands off me. "I think we've been at this long enough. Time you went to bed."

I'd been thinking of the Birdies all over Rob's big sinewy body and how he'd just let them touch him like it didn't mean anything. Maybe if I'd sat down there with him, he'd have let me, too. Maybe he'd have touched my back. "Come on, Alec. Don't stop. Give me a massage and I'll show you my ass." I guess I grabbed him and pulled him onto the sofa, because the next thing I knew, he was rubbing my chest. I leaned back and helped him unbutton my shirt. He started running his finger around my nipples. "Feels good," I groaned. It had been a long time since someone had touched me like that, gently, carefully, not like Tony who must have thought he was wadding up spitballs or something. I was really getting turned on. I pulled at my belt. ''Come on, I'll show you my ass.'' He leaned over and licked my chest. I was about ready to split the seams of my pants. I reached for his crotch and started to rub it. ''Come on, Alec, you wanna see my ass, show me that cock of yours. Show me that great big humongous cock I keep hearing all about. Why should I be the only one in town who's never seen it?''

He stopped what he was doing and straightened up. ''Fuck you, fuck you, fuck you,'' he shouted and stormed into his room, slamming the door behind him.

SCENE XX

Little Me

I woke up around five the next afternoon. I was lying on my bed with my clothes on and had no idea how or when I'd gotten there. Once I got my bearings I went out to the living room. The place was like a tomb, no stereo, no singing, no banging of pots and pans. I had a foggy recollection of having pulled myself out of bed and crawling to the phone to call the store. If I hadn't, well, it was too late now. I made some coffee and a peanut butter sandwich and tried to piece together as much as I could remember from the night before, which was more than enough to know what a fuck-up I'd been. I had no idea where Alec was or when he'd be back, or what I'd say to him, so I sat and stared into space, drinking coffee and hoping he wasn't too bad off. And wondering if my headache would ever go away.

Thinking only made it worse, but I couldn't help going over in my mind what had happened. Sure, I'd drunk too much, and Alec had started it, what with that massage and all. And you couldn't blame me if it felt good. But what had me confused was that deep down inside, I'd wanted it to go further. And it was only my clumsy attempt to make it happen that had prevented it. I don't care how drunk I was, if some real toad, say Harold, for instance, had been pawing me, I would have put a stop to it. Fast. And it's not like Alec isn't attractive. Not, "Oh, my God, I've got to run around the block to get another look at that guy'' attractive, but in his own way. . . . I especially liked the way the hair grew on the back of his neck — little swirls on both sides that disappeared under his collar. I'd noticed them during my neck phase. Once I came up behind him when he was standing at the sink, and for an instant I thought how much I'd like to trace those little swirls with my tongue. Of course I didn't consider actually doing it. I mean, there are limits you don't cross, because once you do, you can't go back. So as far as the night before went, Alec could go on thinking I was just drunk. But I knew it hadn't only been that, and *that* had me worried . . . .

The phone rang around eight. ''Hello, handsome hunk,'' Harold gushed. ''What are you doing home on a Saturday night? Waiting for me to call?''

''What do you want, Harold?''

''Oh, baby, you know what I want. What say I come over and tell you about it. Better yet, I'll show you.''

''Alec's not here.''

''All the better to eat you, my dear.''

''Goodbye, Harold.'' Once I felt confident that he didn't know it was me in that tea room, I forgot that I'd resolved to be nicer to him. I started to hang up.

''Joe, wait! Do you know when he'll be back? I simply *must* talk to him.''

''I have no idea where he went or when he's coming home.''

''You two have a lovers' spat? You been mistreating him again?''

''What are you talking about?''

''You know you're not very nice to Alec, you insensitive brute. And he thinks the world of you.''

''I doubt that very much.''

"My, we *are* in a mood. All right, I give up. But *please* tell him to call me as soon as he gets in."

I hung up the phone, grabbed my coffee mug, and continued to stare into space. On a scale of 1 to 10, I was feeling about 0.2. I tried to get interested in a movie on TV, but I was really listening for Alec's key in the door. When he hadn't turned up by 11:30, I gave in and went to bed. I must have been more passed out than asleep the night before, because my belt buckle had made a deep crease in my stomach and my entire left side ached, so getting comfortable was no easy chore. I hoped the crease would be gone before I met Jerry on Monday. Not to mention the pain. It would sure take the bloom off our first ecstatic encounter if my whole left side was still numb.

I was awakened around 10 the next morning by the good smells coming from the kitchen. I was nervous about facing Alec, so I took my time getting dressed. When I finally left my room he was sitting at the table over a fantastic mushroom omelet. He glanced at me then went back to his breakfast.

"Hello, Alec." He look at me again. "You, uh, out late last night?"

"Don't talk to me."

I poured myself some coffee and sat down at the table. "Alec?"

"There's half an omelet in the pan if you're hungry."

I helped myself and sat back down. Things couldn't be all that bad, if he cooked for me. "Alec?"

"I said don't talk to me."

We sat there chewing, my every swallow sounding like a tidal wave in the silence. "Alec?"

"What do you want?"

"About the other night."

"Forget it."

"I can't forget it. We started out having a good time, celebrating your promotion, then I ruined it."

"The whole thing was a mistake. You were drunk."

"Maybe. But I still shouldn't have done what I did or said what I said."

"What difference does it make?"

"Alec, I'm trying to apologize."

"For what? You wanna see my cock, I'll show you my cock. You want a picture of it, you can take a picture of it. A portrait. Alec the prick. That's me."

"That's not true and you know it."

"If you say so."

"What about your promotion? Remember? They like your work. They like you."

"Lucky me, Connie Career, the best little record seller in town."

"Stop putting yourself down. You deserved that promotion — and more! Just look how talented you are — you should be in that show, not just watching from the side. You should be on the stage, in the spotlight."

"That's my life. All singing, all dancing."

"I'm trying hard to make you feel better. To apologize."

"You're forgiven. Drop it."

"Where did you go last night?"

"What the fuck business is it of yours?"

"You were out pretty late, that's all."

"I *hope* all your worrying about me didn't keep you from your beauty sleep. Are you intact? Every muscle in place? Did you inspect yourself in the mirror? Flex every little tendon?"

"I've felt better."

"Drinking and narcissism don't mix."

"If you must know I feel rotten. My belt buckle dug into my stomach so I'm almost bleeding and I ache so much

I'll have to go easy on the weights tomorrow."

He laughed. " 'Ooh, do you love you.' " I'd heard his *Superman* record enough to know where *that* line came from, and I took his singing as a good sign.

"By the way, Harold wants you to call him."

"This must be my lucky day."

"He said it was important."

He didn't move so I got up and started washing the dishes. I couldn't tell how mad he was. Sometimes I had the feeling he enjoyed his bad moods, a chance to play a different role. When I finished in the kitchen I heard him on the phone with Harold. When he hung up he was mad. This time, for real.

"Great. Just great. Harold gets a big opportunity, another chance to play the star, so he comes running to me for help. Alec the doormat. You need someone to dump on? Here's Alec. You need a favor? Here's Alec. You need someone to write your review, organize your radio show? Just get in line."

"What radio show?"

"Harold." He waved his hand in the direction of the phone. "The campus station wants him to do a weekly music show."

"What does he need you for? There's nothing hard about a radio show. First you play one side of the record, then the other."

"It's not that easy. The station has a fabulous collection of show albums, some rare stuff. I've tried to buy the whole thing — some for the store, some for me. They've been sitting around unused for years. How many college kids want to hear show tunes? But I guess they know what they've got — now they're trying to expand their audience, attract people in town, maybe even in the city. So they call Harold, local media star, and ask him to work up a show with a new angle. 'Harold

Waldman on Broadway' they want to call it. Who else but me is going to give him ideas?''

''Don't do it.''

''What?''

''You heard me. For once let Harold sink or swim on his own.''

''The idea is not unappealing. But I can't.''

''Why not?''

''Look, a lot of people like Harold because he's a character. He's outrageous, and people accept that as long as he laughs at himself. But the fact that he's a flaming queen is not exactly a secret. There are people who are just waiting for him to stumble, waiting to crucify the faggot. Harold is a very visible faggot, and as long as he can come up with some legitimate ideas once in a while, no one can touch him. Let him slip up and the vultures will get him. And don't think he doesn't know it. He's been scared more than once. Really scared. So I have to help him.''

''He's not worth it.''

''Harold is OK.''

''You're loyal to your friends, aren't you?''

''I don't have many.''

''Alec, I'm really sorry about the other night.''

''I know you are. Forget it.''

''Do I mistreat you?''

''What do you mean?''

''Last night, when I spoke to Harold, he said I mistreat you. Do I?''

''You just act like yourself. You can't help it.''

''What does that mean?''

He sighed. ''Joe, you're vain, shallow, and intolerant. But you're showing signs of improving, and basically, you're rather sweet.''

''You think so?'' I decided to pass on ''shallow'' and concentrate on ''sweet.''

"Underneath that muscle-bound exterior there beats the heart of a wimp."

"Alec!"

"You asked, didn't you? And another thing — were you trying to make up to me, or did you mean what you said, about me being smart and talented?"

"Sure I meant it."

He started singing to me, snatches of lyrics from songs like "Deep Down Inside," "Very Nice Man," and "I Like you." I sure hoped *he* meant it.

SCENE XXI

The Boy Friend

Alec spent the rest of the day working on ideas for Harold's radio program. It would be a cinch, he decided; just organize each show around songs that followed a theme. His own record collection was a gold mine.

"There are songs about *everything*," he told me, "about people, places, things. I can think of half a dozen songs about money, more about the joys of being rich. I made a list of songs about getting married and thought of a whole bunch more about *not* getting married. I'll bet I could do a whole hour just using duets by people who hate each other. And the songs about dances — everything from the New-Fangled Tango and the Spanish Panic to the Walla Walla Boola and the Kangaroo. And think about who's been in Broadway shows. How many people know that Vivien Leigh starred in a musical? Shelley Winters? Julie Harris, Melvyn Douglas — even Farley Granger! The possibilities are endless. It's like the game we always play, pick a word and see how many songs it's in. Free associate. Only an idiot like Harold would think this was hard."

So he was getting Harold off the hook, again. It burned me up the way he let himself be used by that halfwit, but he was so happy writing down his lists of songs that I was relieved to see him back to his usual self and not mad at me. Because I was in a good mood, too. I was determined to be in top shape for my meeting with Jerry the next morning, and I spent the afternoon getting ready. I went to the gym for a light exercise routine to work out some of my aches and sat in the sauna for a full half-hour. At home I gave myself a close inspection in the mirror, which was lucky since I squeezed out what might have turned into a zit on my shoulder. I did the best I could with my feet, but I still had the remains of one black toenail that I hoped Jerry wouldn't notice. I also decided a last jerk-off would be OK, too, since I didn't want to be too quick on the trigger the next day, and I'd have the whole night to rest up and replenish. So all in all, Alec and I both had productive afternoons. By suppertime, when he served a poached salmon in *beurre rouge*, we'd forgotten our disastrous encounter two nights before.

I was excited the next morning. I'd already picked out my post-workout clothes, black Levis and a green Lacoste. I'd read a book on how to choose your colors, and that green was definitely me. I decided I'd really get Jerry going if I wore something hot at the gym, and after trying on a dozen outfits, I finally chose a sleeveless blue top with the running shorts Alec had told me drove guys crazy. I didn't plan to wear socks; guys in shorts without socks always look half-undressed, and it makes your legs look longer, gives a nice line to your calf muscles. Jerry always had a slow, hot shower and shave, which I knew would give me time to get myself into peak form. So along with my usual shampoo, conditioner, moisturizer, and after-shave, I went the extra mile and packed baby oil and body musk.

Alec was a little hyper about starting his first full day in his new job, so he whipped up some of his famous French toast, accompanied by a rousing rendition of "Nothing Can Stop Me Now." I don't usually like a heavy meal before I work out, but French toast is, after all, a mixture of carbohydrates and protein, so I had just a couple of pieces. We left together, wishing each other luck.

I wanted to make sure I got to the gym early, before Jerry, to give myself time to comb my hair and make sure my clothes looked just right. I did some stretching to limber up, and I was relieved to find that most of the pain was gone from my left side. If he noticed the bruise from my belt buckle, I'd say something cute, tease him a little, tell him it was a hicky.

He arrived about fifteen minutes later, and while he signed in, I put my arms over my head, grabbing one wrist with the other hand and bending side to side, a move I'd watched him do that always looked great and showed off a guy's legs.

''Joe, my man, don't start without me,'' he shouted on his way into the locker room. I was so excited I was afraid I'd get sweat stains on my shirt, so I put my hands on my hips and did some waist bends to create a little breeze and dry my pits — sweat is only sexy after you've been exercising, not when your workout buddy first lays eyes on you. Jerry came out looking fabulous, and all I could think was if people thought Tony and I made a perfect pair, wait till they saw me and Jerry.

We started in on the machines. I was working on the double chest machine, what we called the pec deck, and Jerry was telling me about being weighed under water.

''It's the only way to determine how much body fat you have,'' he explained. ''I tested out at only 10 percent — almost as good as a marathon runner.''

''You've got a great build, Jer,'' I grunted as I started the decline press.

''You should talk,'' he grinned. ''You're the envy of the locker room.'' He slapped me on the shoulder. By then

I'd lost count of my repetitions and did more than usual. Which was lucky, since my throbbing temples covered up the fact that I was blushing.

We had just moved to the mats to start our lifting when I glanced in the mirror and almost dropped dead then and there. A large, square figure, looking horribly familiar, was talking to the instructor at the desk.

"Joe, is that you?" Judy came running toward me. There was no place to hide.

"Judy, what the hell are you doing here?"

"What do you think? I want to get in shape. Find out if there's a figure under here. It's that surprise I was telling you about. Can you show me around?"

"I definitely can *not* show you around. That's why they have people working here."

"Yeah," she giggled, nodding toward the instructor, "but his body isn't half as nice as yours. Why not have the best?" She gave me a big smile and looked me over from head to toe. I suddenly felt naked and exposed and wished at the very least I'd worn socks.

"It's against the rules. You have to have a regular instructor show you around. So I'll see you later."

"It sure was a coincidence meeting you here."

I'll just bet, I thought to myself. Jerry had been tightening the weights on the bar during all this, and after she'd gone he gave me a big wink. "Quite the lady-killer, eh, Joe?"

The last I saw of Judy she was getting strapped into the lower back and hip machine, looking like a beached whale trying to ride a bicycle. I forced myself not to glance her way again; she'd already spoiled what was supposed to have been a great workout.

"So what do ya say, Joe?" Jerry said as we headed for the locker room. "Ready for that breakfast now?"

There were other guys around, but standing just a few

feet from Jerry in the shower, both of us naked, I started to get hard. I turned the water on as hot as I could stand and faced the wall. That did the trick, and besides, I figured the hot water would give my skin a sexy glow. When I caught up with Jerry he was lathering up his face at a sink, telling someone one of his jokes, something about the sheep-herder's theme song, "ewe, ewe, ewe, I'm in love with ewe, ewe, ewe." Pretty soon he had the attention of everyone there. So he told them about the farmer's daughter, half-girl, half-sheep. "Her tail got in the way, but at least she kept the grass clipped." You had to hand it to Jerry, he sure was a friendly guy.

By the time he finished with his jokes I'd had a chance to dry my hair and rub myself all over with baby oil, then pat on some musk at all my pulse points. We left the locker room together, only to be confronted by Judy hoisting herself into the sit-up machine.

"See you at the store, Joe. You wait and see, I'll be beautiful yet!"

Jerry looked at me and laughed. "She reminds me of a joke. . . ."

On our way to the restaurant we made small talk about our training and the progress we were making. After we'd ordered, he started telling me again about that body-fat test. Hydrostatic weighing, he called it. He knew where I could have it done for twenty bucks.

"See, Joe, a lot of guys fall into the trap of thinking that just because they *look* good, they're in perfect health. I'm not saying there's anything wrong with you, of course, considering the great shape you're in, but it's interesting to get the statistics."

"I'll think about it."

"You should. I mean, a guy wants to be healthy." I

wasn't sure where this conversation was headed, but as long as it was about the shape I was in, it seemed OK. "You don't smoke, do you Joe?" I shook my head. "Drink much?"

I waited for the waitress to serve our breakfasts. "I lift a beer or two, you know, when I'm out somewhere. Wine with dinner sometimes." I figured it was time to be a little cute. "I may have my vices, Jer, but drinking isn't one of them." He didn't pick up on it.

"Good, real good," was all he said. What was this, a compatibility test? "Got a girlfriend?" I thought we were past the point where he'd have to ask that, but he must have thought I was so butch I went both ways. I shook my head again. "Come on, Joe, a great-looking guy like you? I saw the way that chick back at the gym looked you over. They must line up at your door."

"I don't encourage them." I was a little confused by his line of questioning.

"Old hard to get, huh? You devil. But listen, Joe, even if you don't have a girlfriend, it won't be long before you do, and eventually you'll want to get married. I know, I know, don't look at me like that, guys like us, sure, we mess around, try this and that, but face it, in the long run we all get hooked by some little piece who turns out to have more on the ball than a good ass."

"I'm not sure I know what you're talking about, Jer."

"What I'm talking about, Joe, my man, is the future. Your future, my future. And planning for it. What I'm talking about, Joe, is life insurance."

"Huh?"

"You see, Joe, this is the time to think about it. While you're young and healthy. Now I can offer you a wider range of options than you ever thought possible. At a price you can afford. Believe me."

"Huh?"

"I kid you not, Joe. Here, let me get a prospectus out of my gym bag. I can explain it all to you in no time."

Just about then the remains of Alec's French toast, which had been sitting happily at the very bottom of my stomach, started doing a 180-degree turn in an effort to trade places with the salsa from the Mexican omelet I'd just finished. The cottage fries were sandwiched in between and trying to get out in whatever direction they could. Jerry was showing me charts and graphs and talking about life expectancy and my insides were churning. When he stopped for air, I looked at him.

"Is that what this breakfast is all about? Selling me life insurance?"

"I wouldn't be trying if it wasn't for your own good, Joe."

"Look, Jerry, I'm feeling a little queasy. Too much grease in the potatoes, I think. Here's a few bucks — I have to get some fresh air." I threw the money on the table, grabbed my gym stuff and made for the door, ignoring Jerry's attempts to call me back. I was really afraid I was going to throw up, so I went around the corner and sat on a park bench, looking for the nearest clump of bushes I could hide in if I had to toss my breakfast.

After a few deep breaths, my stomach settled some, and harsh reality began to set it. First I got mad, good and mad at that bastard. Then I started going through the I-should-have-saids. I should have said, "What kind of shit spends weeks getting to know a guy so he can spring a sales pitch on him? What kind of guy feels up your muscles, talks you into buddy exercises, tells you how good-looking you are, just to flatter you so you'll pull out the old checkbook?" The more I thought about it, the more I knew the answer. A guy who's the life of the party, everybody's friend, the locker-room clown. A guy like Jerry, with his sick jokes, his easy grin, his fancy clothes. Jerry was more than your typical slick salesman, he was an actor, as good as any of Alec's friends. And so much like them, always preening, showing himself off, playing to an audience. He was good, all right, good enough to fool a horny, hard-up idiot like me. *Me* — such a good judge of character! I'd been completely taken in by a smile in the mirror and a wink my way. And I'd been so damn *sure* of him. Wasn't there anyone a guy could trust? It was just like grandma used to say, "When God gives us flour, the devil steals the sack." Well, I'd learned one thing — the devil wore Italian seamless racing pants. And favored turquoise. I almost had to laugh.

At least until I realized where that left me. No Tony, no Jerry, no possibilities, no sex. Was it back to the tea room and Harold waving money at me under the partition? Long nights at the bar wondering who was gossiping about me, staying up half the night in the hope there'd be a party I wouldn't be invited to unless Alec arranged it? Or was I going to stay home and spend my life with Alec and the Birdies trying to think up show tunes with the word "misery" in them? And all the while doing my best to avoid this lesbian who was following me all over town urging me to "confess" so she could initiate me into the sisterhood. If I hadn't had to walk clear across town to get home, I'd have gone behind a bush and barfed just on principle.

I don't have to spell out what kind of mood I was in the rest of the day. And Judy sure didn't help. She was all excited about beginning her Nautilus workouts.

"You watch, Joe, give me a few months and you're going to see a new me."

"I can wait."

"I know, you don't think I can do it. But I'm on a

diet, and with regular exercise. . . . How come you didn't introduce me to your friend?''

''He's not my friend. I just work out with him. Or used to, sometimes. You need someone to spot you.''

''I sure had the two of you spotted.''

''Meaning?''

''Just that you were the two best-looking guys in the place. It seemed right, somehow, that the two of you would be together.''

So she thought she had us figured out, did she? So she wanted to meet Jerry? Maybe I should introduce them. Let him turn on the charm and take *her* out to breakfast sometime. See how she liked his asinine sheep jokes. I just glared at her.

''You're in quite a mood, aren't you?''

''Leave me alone, Judy, I'm having a bad day.''

''Anything you want to talk about?''

''No.''

''Did you have a fight with your friend? You two were real chummy when you left together.''

''Drop it, Judy.''

''OK, OK.'' She started to walk away then turned around. ''Joe?'' I gave her an annoyed look, but her skin was thick in addition to being ample. ''You sure looked cute in your gym outfit.''

''It's not an 'outfit.' It's clothes, just clothes. You have to be comfortable.''

''Whatever. You still looked great. So did your friend. I guess you're not supposed to do that at the gym, I mean, look over the other people like that.''

''You're supposed to work out.'' Which is all I planned to do from then on. And *not* when I knew Jerry would be there.

''Maybe you could help me out. What did you call it, spot me?''

"That's only for lifting weights, not the machines. Those you do alone. Quietly, fast, and in order. Don't go jumping from machine to machine. It bugs people."

"Sure. Thanks for the tip. Anything else you can tell me?"

"Just to leave me alone. Please."

"Sorry. But if it's anything you want to discuss, I can be very understanding."

"I'll keep it in mind." Fortunately we got busy right then and I was able to slip away and show some guy a tennis racket. But Judy kept hovering around me the rest of the day, trying, I suppose, to look "understanding." It was all I could do, with her watching me, to think up a way to display some new camouflage sweats. I ended up having to stay late till I was satisfied it all looked right. When I got home the apartment was empty and there was no dinner waiting, so there was nothing to do but make a peanut butter sandwich and kill time till Alec got home.

I'd be glad when that damned show he was working on would be over so things could get back to normal — dinner on time, someone around I could tell my troubles to. But the play was two weeks off, and Alec still didn't know where he stood with Kelly. Just a few days before we'd both thought we were on the verge of finding Mr. Right. I wondered if he was going to be in for as big a shock as I was.

When he finally got home he was bubbling. They'd given him a lot of responsibility in his new job at the store and Kelly had said something nice to him at the rehearsal, so I just sat there looking glum and waiting for him to notice and ask what was wrong. Eventually I gave up and went to bed and tried to beat off. But I couldn't get a good fantasy going. Jerry automatically came to mind first, but picturing him just got me mad. I tried getting off on that dancer friend of Alec's, Rob, but all I could see were the Birdies pawing him. I even thought about Bud, my boss, and his muscular forearms, but I kept seeing Judy's face peering over my shoulder. As for Tony, well, the less I thought about him these days, the better. I laid my hand over my shrunken cock and tried to figure out how a great-looking hunk like me had come to such a dead end. One thing was clear, nothing was working out the way I'd planned.

SCENE XXII

Here's Love

I was in no mood to contemplate facing Jerry again, so I changed my schedule at the gym. I'd also made up my mind to forget lifting weights and stick with the machines. Sure, I'd gained some muscle and looked pretty fabulous, but I didn't think I had anyone to look fabulous for, and that heavy lifting always did make me a little nervous. The machines isolate the muscles more than lifting does, so I had to lower some of the weights; even so the old pains set in again. Judy was going through the same agony I was, only she was proud of it, couldn't wait to tell me which machine made her hurt where. At least it distracted her from trying to uncover my feminine side. As long as she didn't bug me, I didn't mind her being around. With Alec gone all the time, I was even glad to have *someone* to talk to, even if it had to be Judy.

I had to hand it to her, she was sticking to her new regimen, yogurt for lunch instead of running across the street to the bakery, an apple on her break instead of cookies. I suspected she was doing all this for some woman, making herself over for some hairy-legged libber, another volleyball freak. Or maybe she was hot for some bodybuilder, one of the female Rambo types who pumped iron along with the guys. I didn't dare ask; I figured she'd be only too glad to tell me. As long as we limited our conversations to work and working out, she wasn't so bad.

During one of our increasingly rare dinners together Alec told me I probably wouldn't want to be home the next Sunday night — he was having a party for some of his close friends. I was pretty starved for company, even if it meant that bunch, and I almost told him I'd like to go. Maybe Rob would be there and I could get a better look at him — without Tom and Randy all over him. Who knows, I might even talk to *them* if that's all I was offered. But I changed my mind as soon as he told me the theme of the get-together.

"It's an Ethel Merman memorial. She was born in January, but too many people are out of town then. She died in February, but that's too depressing. Her two biggest hits, *Annie Get Your Gun* and *Gypsy* both opened in May, so we figured that was a good time for a party. It's become a tradition. Everyone comes as a character from one of her shows. I'm going to wear this buckskin number, you know, with fringe, and boots — Annie, of course. Not original, but easy. Randy's looking in all the second-hand shops to find a nice padded suit so he can be Mama Rose, and I suppose Tom will be Gypsy herself. Harold wants to come as Dolly. The show was written with Ethel in mind and she did play in it for nine months, but the real reason is that he's got a fabulous sequined gown he loves to wear. Someone is bound to come as Mme. DuBarry and there's always a Panama Hattie. We show videos of her old movies. *Call Me Madam* is a gem, and we even have a tape of the butchered TV version of *Anything Goes.*"

Just hearing about this little to-do was enough to make me grateful that he'd warned me. I didn't understand how someone like him, usually so sensible, could wear a dress and think it was fun.

"Of course," he went on, more to himself at this point than to me, "Harold might surprise us. He can get clothes for any part because he wears the same size as his mother, and she has closets full. You should have seen him at our Tony party when we were pulling for *La Cage.* We had a salute to Jerry Herman; Harold came as Molly Picon in *Milk and Honey*."

The thought of Harold dressed up as a woman, dressed up as a man, *un*dressed — was enough to convince me I didn't want to be anywhere near the apartment that night. I volunteered to fill in for one of the guys at the store that Sunday and figured I'd grab a hamburger and go to a movie. Maybe even stop in at the Alamo and try to find someone who *wasn't* into Ethel Merman.

We'd had a miserable April that year, cloudy and cold, with snow into the third week. That Sunday was the first warm day; it finally felt like spring. The store was mobbed, but Judy and I worked together and managed to keep the lines moving. Whatever her faults, she was a good worker, and we even joked around a little, which helped us get through the busy afternoon. When we closed at five it was still warm, so I wandered around the mall for a while trying to decide where to eat. Then in a store window I saw Judy's reflection right behind me. Great, she'd been following me. That's what I get for being nice to her.

"What's up, Joe? Not rushing off to get home for once?"

"I'm in no hurry."

"Want to grab a bite?"

"Sure, why not?" It was better than eating alone and would help me kill time. Besides, I hadn't minded Judy for the last few days, she hadn't been making a pest of herself. "I was going to have a hamburger or something."

"Oh. I'd like that, but I'm on a strict diet and I have to be careful. I was thinking more like a salad."

"Whatever."

"Where do you want to go?"

"Anyplace is fine."

She looked at me like she was trying to make up her mind about something. "How about my place? I could throw something together in no time."

Shit. "Don't bother. I'll grab a sandwich."

"It's just a couple of blocks. I've got a refrigerator full of lettuce and stuff — sprouts, seeds. It wouldn't take more than a minute."

I knew how persistent she could be and I wasn't in the mood to argue. What the hell, if she was going to spring some confession on me, better it not be in public. As we were walking over to her place I was struck by the fear that I might be confronted by some jealous lesbian who'd give me dirty looks and pounce on me every time I opened my mouth. "Got a roommate, Judy?"

"Not now," she said, with a strange grin, "but I'm working on it."

Frankly, I didn't see how two people could ever live in her apartment; it was hardly more than a single room. At least she'd done it up OK, no women's lib posters or those anti-men slogans stuck to the refrigerator door like I'd seen in some girls' kitchens. It's hard to warm up to a woman who advertises she's a ball buster.

Judy cleared the table of some books, mainly phys. ed. texts, reminding me that volleyballs were the only balls she planned to get her hands on. "Make yourself at home while I step into the kitchen." She smiled and took about three steps to the sink. "There's a book on the sofa you might want to look at, all about Nautilus training. I thought if I'm going to do it, I might as well do it right."

I settled into the sofa while she puttered in the kitchen. I thumbed through the book, a typical workout guide where some guy who's probably been lifting weights for ten years sits in a machine with a big smile on his face, as if you could get to look like him by exercising twenty minutes a day a couple of times a week. I know how hard it is, and you sure don't smile. Of course I always enjoy the pictures, because the men are always gorgeous and never have much on — makes you wonder who these books are really intended for. They usually manage to work in a shot or two of some guy losing his swimsuit, still smiling, or a group sitting in a steam room with strategically draped towels. Now the smiles on *their* faces I can believe. Some of these books even give the models' names. Fuckin' guys must get fan mail by the ton.

I was so absorbed by a photo of a hairy-chested blond laughing his way through the torso arm pull-down that I didn't even realize Judy was standing next to me, holding out a glass of wine.

"Quite a hunk, isn't he?" There she was, already trying to draw me out. This was going to be even worse than I thought.

"Well he didn't get that way using the machine. He's a lifter."

"Like you?"

"I, uh, haven't been doing much of that lately; I'm not sure I like it. You can get hurt."

"Is that why you work out with a friend."

"If you can find one."

"I haven't seen you at the gym this week, not since the first day."

"I go different times. Depends on my schedule — it's different every day."

"Oh. That guy, the good-looking one you were working out with when I saw you, he said you're usually like clockwork, same time every day. He wondered where you are, too."

"You've been talking to Jerry?" Wouldn't she leave me alone?

"Just asking for you. And I had a couple of questions about the machines."

"That's what the help is there for." I was afraid I'd have to start timing my workouts to dodge both Judy and Jerry. Was there no end to my misery?

She served the salad. She didn't have any bread, so I had to nibble some low-cal crackers that tasted like salted cardboard. She told me about her diet, and I pretended to be interested, wondering why I'd agreed to all this and where I'd go later for a hamburger. Luckily she found some ice cream hidden in the back of the freezer and assured me I'd be doing her a favor if I finished it, which I did. Then she made some coffee and sat down at the end of the sofa. There wasn't anyplace else to sit, so I took the other end, leaving as much room between us as possible. She was determined to tell me about her self-improvement plan, while I sat there trying to dislodge assorted seeds from my teeth with my tongue.

"I've never really minded being . . .big . . .like this," she was telling me. "Never gave it a second thought. But you know how it is these days, everyone's into fitness, and if you don't look like you're barely surviving anorexia, you just don't fit the mold. Not to mention muscles. A lot of the women in my phys. ed. classes pump iron." I grunted "uh huh" whenever I thought she expected me to say something. "So I decided I'd give it a try. I'll never be skinny. I'm a big girl. Bone structure. But I'll see what I can do."

She looked at me, waiting. "Good for you," I mumbled. I was about to ask for a toothpick, but I decided this was a job that was going to require a complete flossing.

"I'll tell you something funny, Joe." She sort of unwedged herself from the corner of the sofa where she'd started out and leaned toward me. "Not everyone is turned off by big women." She looked at me again, to gauge my reaction. I stared into my lap. "Oh, yes, it's a well-kept secret, but a lot of guys like 'em well-rounded."

Yeah, I thought to myself, and a lot of women, too. "Oh?"

"Really. You'd be amazed." I wasn't sure, but it seemed she was even closer to me now. I figured I'd better start paying attention. "When I was a kid, well, not really a kid, I mean thirteen or fourteen, old enough to *know*," she paused, but I just waited her out. "We had this neighbor, right next door. Nice guy, in his early thirties, but to a kid, you know, he seemed old. He was a Cadillac dealer, so he always had a brand new Caddy. Every Sunday, week in and week out, he'd wash those great big cars. Sometimes he'd let me help him. Once he said he had to pull the car into the garage, out of the sun, to polish it, and asked me if I wanted to clean the inside. But first he had to show me how. Climbed right in after me. Had his hand up my shirt in no time."

I guess that this was what had turned her off to men. That happens, sometimes, when girls are molested. At least I supposed so. "What'd you do?"

She leaned even closer, and I couldn't help noticing that there were only a few inches between us on the sofa. "Why, I *let* him. I liked it. And that wasn't the last time. Seems that car needed polishing more and more often, especially when his wife left for church." There were no inches between us. "Once I even put my hand down his pants and *felt* it."

I was beginning to get that same sick feeling I'd had earlier in the week with Jerry. What saved me was the fact that there wasn't enough in my stomach to cause me much grief, just a few lettuce leaves cooling under the ice cream. I pushed myself back into the arm of the sofa. She was getting closer and closer, this great mountain of girl oozing toward me.

"I guess what I'm trying to say, Joe, is that I've always known."

"Known what?"

"That I've got this voracious appetite for men. I guess you could say I'm a nymphomaniac. A textbook case."

I had the feeling I was about to be engulfed like a banana in a jello salad. I jumped to my feet. "Listen, thanks for dinner, but I really have to get going. I'm expecting a phone call."

She wasn't ruffled. "It's OK, I understand, Joe. You're a hot dude. At first I thought you were just another dumb jock, like all those other assholes at the store, but then I saw the real you. The sweet, sensitive you. I'm a sucker for sensitive men."

Her choice of words had me really nervous. "You've got me all wrong."

She shook her head. "I tell you, I *know* you, Joe."

"I'm not sensitive. I'm not even nice. My roommate always tells me I'm narrow-minded and pompous. Look, I really gotta go."

"Sure, Joe, sure. But you just wait. Give me a couple of months. Diet, exercise, and I'm letting my hair grow. You're going to get hooked on me, you irresistable hunk. And I'll make sure it was worth waiting for."

I'll wait, all right, I told myself as I ran down the stairs from her apartment. I'll wait till the cactuses grow cocks. It had gotten cold out and I didn't have a jacket. I jogged a few blocks to a movie theater and went in without even knowing what was playing. It didn't matter. All I could think about was my rotten luck. Talk about bad weeks. "For every valley, there are two mountains," grandma used to say. Well, I felt like I'd been over the Alps. First that drunken fiasco with Alec, then my major miscalculation with Jerry, now this disaster with Judy. Who, I was sure, I had all figured out. And it turns out that all along she was hot to get into my pants and *feel* it. Jeez. Now I'd never be rid of her. Dear God, why couldn't she just have been a lesbian?

It was only 9:30 when the movie ended; I didn't have the patience to wait through the intermission for the part I'd missed. I knew Alec's party would be in full swing, so I ran up the hill to the Alamo. The place was packed, but it was much too early for the gay crowd to have arrived. At least the body heat would warm me up. I was making my way to the bar when I caught the sound of a familiar voice — "Hear about the sheepherder's wife? B-a-a-arbra-a-a." Then I saw him, sitting at a table with another guy, trying to hold the attention of a couple of college girls. It figured, Jerry'd be just the type that comes to the Alamo to hit on coeds. Probably invites them over to his place to see his mortality tables.

I turned back to the door, took a deep breath and plunged into the cold night. So this was what my life had come to, a ping-pong ball bouncing back and forth between Jerry and Judy, one trying to get my money, the other waiting to eat me alive. Tell me, Jer, you got a policy to cover that?

SCENE XXIII

Stop the World

There was nothing to do but go home and face another scene I was hardly in the mood for. I didn't hear any shrieking laughter from out on the landing, but the sight that greeted me seemed to strike the right note of absurdity. Seven or eight people of indeterminate sex, mustaches and feathers, beards and boas. Send in the clowns. I was able to pick out Harold, because he was yapping away, and Tom, by his beak nose, but the rest could have been anyone for all I knew. Except in the big chair, wearing a ruffled white shirt and black pants — Rob. I couldn't tell if he was in a costume or not, he always dressed a little different, anyway. I thought for sure he looked my way as I hurried to my room, but just then a favorite song began and they all started singing along.

I stayed hidden for about an hour, lamenting my fate and inspecting my nose in the mirror for clogged pores. Not that it mattered. I might as well have turned into one big zit — there was no one who cared how I looked, no one to look good for. I hadn't had much dinner, and I knew Alec had spent the day in the kitchen preparing for the party, so after I heard the door open and close a few times and good-byes being said, I decided it might be safe to go out and scrounge some food. Alec was in the kitchen with Randy, cleaning up. Tom was talking to Harold, and Rob was still there, listening to them with that half-smile of his.

Harold hadn't changed out of his dress, and I couldn't help thinking what the newspaper or TV station would do if he was picked up like that on the street. Tom had put on his regular clothes but had his makeup on, so he looked even more ridiculous than he had before. Rob looked the same — terrific. I strolled by him into the kitchen and found some cheese and dip in the refrigerator, but the crackers were still in the living room, so I brought the trays in there.

"We missed you, handsome," Harold called to me.

"I tried, Harold, but I didn't miss you."

"He's such a tease," he said to Tom. "Isn't he a tease? He'd love to get under my petticoat, but the boy is just *too* shy."

Tom got up and went off to find Randy. I knew that once Harold turned the conversation to me he wasn't interested. He didn't like me, and I knew why. I almost began to wish I'd been a little nicer to him and Randy. Maybe I'd have run into Rob a lot sooner if I hadn't always given them the cold shoulder. I still hadn't met Rob, not officially, and I sure didn't expect Harold to further my cause. He was fluffing up his skirt and smiling at me.

"Ooh, he's got food. Bring it over here, honey, where Rob and I can get at it. And bring the food, too!" I moved the tray to the coffee table. I didn't mind getting closer to Rob. Harold took a piece of cheese and looked it over before popping it into his mouth. "This is cold, and I'm in the mood for something *hot.* Come closer, Joe, this is no whalebone making my skirt stand out."

"Don't you ever give up, Harold?"

"Of course not. You just have to get to know me. To know me is to love me. Then again, you can love me without knowing me, too. It wouldn't be the first time. Don't worry, Joe, I'm patient. I can wait."

It seemed everyone was waiting for me. They might as well take a number, the line forms to the rear. Judy and

Harold and Jerry with his prospectus. Judy could feel it, Jerry could insure it, and Harold could review it.

Harold got up, as he put it, to go pee pee, and I was finally left alone with Rob. I'd never said a word to the guy, never even heard him talk. I was almost afraid to, he'd probably turn out to be a swish like the others. He was looking at me, so I decided the time had come. "So how were the films?"

"OK. It was just an excuse for a party."

"So how was the party?"

He smiled. "Like every other party."

"Is that a costume?"

The smile turned into a laugh. He had a nice laugh, though I wasn't sure what he thought was funny. "Yes, it's a costume. I'm supposed to be an unemployed duke — Fernando Lamas in *Happy Hunting.* Except I didn't know he and Ethel Merman hated each other till these guys filled me in, so I took off my sash." He pulled a red ribbon from under his chair and smiled at me. "Out of respect for Ethel."

I smiled back. So far, so good. He seemed all right, sounded butch, and hadn't come in a dress. Just then that damned Randy came in looking like his regular self except he was wearing two earrings instead of one. He plopped down on Rob's lap. Gross out time.

"There's no one to take her place," he sighed. "The musical's dead. What're we going to do without musicals, Robbie?"

"I'm sure the theater will survive," he said, "it always does." He didn't seem to mind Randy pawing him, but at least he didn't paw back.

"Randy," Tom said from the kitchen door, "get your buns together and let's make it history." They gathered up their shoes and dresses, put on their coats, and after ten minutes of noisy fussing, kissed Alec on the cheek and gave Rob long, wet kisses.

"Oh, my God," Harold shrieked, coming out of the bathroom. "I'm missing the orgy! Wait for me! Dibs on Joe!"

Fortunately, he'd changed his clothes, but his return sparked another long round of good-byes. He and the Birdies finally left together. Alec took some dirty glasses into the kitchen, and I was alone again with Rob.

"I'm not sure we've ever really met," I said. "I'm Joe."

"I know. And I'm Rob." He shook my hand with a solid grip.

"I guess we've seen each other a few times. You know, around."

"Yeah. Around." I half expected him to bring up Tony then. Everybody else did. This time, I was lucky. "I don't really go out much. This town is not exactly a hotbed of fascinating people."

"Just Tom and Randy?"

He smirked. "They're just kids. They *can* be amusing, when I'm in the mood for this sort of thing, you know, silly parties."

"I suppose they fill you in on all the gossip?"

"I don't have time to waste dishing the dirt."

This guy was sounding better and better. Could it be he was the one person in town who hadn't made it a hobby to pursue the details of my private life? Just then Alec came in.

"I hate to interrupt what I'm sure must be sparkling repartee, but I'm going to bed. Joe, don't forget to put the cheese away and turn out the kitchen light. You forgot the other night."

I hated the way that sounded, like a wife nagging her husband. Rob probably thought Alec and I had something going, like everyone else did. He put on his coat and thanked Alec. Then he shook my hand again.

"I guess I'll see you around," I said.

"Yeah. Around." The smile.

When he was gone I turned to Alec. "I wish you wouldn't talk to me like that, in front of people."

"Like what?"

"Oh, nothing. Forget it."

"Pardon me for living."

"Alec, I'm sorry. I've had a really shitty day. I mean *really* shitty. In fact, I've had a shitty week."

"Wanna talk about it?"

"I just . . . nothing's worked out the way I'd expected. It's too painful to go into." He shrugged and picked up the last of the dirty glasses. When he came back from the kitchen he was holding a couple of snifters and waving the brandy at me. I took a glass. "So how was your party?"

"Good for a few laughs."

"As only dressing up in drag can be."

"Look, if you're going to start in on that again, I'll pass."

"You're right. I'm not up for a fight, either. I'm not up for much of anything."

"Is it that bad?"

"You wouldn't believe it." I sipped my brandy and figured what the hell, I had to talk to someone. So I started from the top — the breakfast with Jerry, the dinner with Judy, and how I'd been so sure I had them both figured out — and been so wrong. When I got to the part about Judy creeping toward me down the sofa, he couldn't hold back the laughter he'd been trying hard to control. "Alec, it's not funny." Then I grinned. "Well, it's not *that* funny."

"I'm sorry, Joe, but you seem to have a knack for getting yourself into things like this. You let people take you in. God knows Tony had you going in circles."

"What do you mean by that?"

"Nothing. It's just that from what you've told me. . . ."

"I think you know a lot more than what I've told you."

"Joe, neither one of us is in the mood to argue, so let's drop it, OK? I might as well finish cleaning up. I'm not really tired anymore."

I went into the bathroom to wash up and brush my teeth. I supposed it *was* pretty funny, what happened with Jerry and Judy. At least it seemed funny then. Things were never so bad after I'd talked them over with Alec. And he was right about not wanting to discuss Tony. The last thing I needed was to get an earful of bar gossip. Hadn't I heard enough of that?

I spit into the sink. I'd better not let myself think about it, about all those lies, it would just get me worked up. But what *did* Alec mean, about Tony having me going in circles? He always knew more than he let on. What *else* did he know? There were still a few pieces missing from the puzzle; maybe it was time to fill them in.

So far, the pieces I had spelled T-O-N, as in the amount of shit that bastard had dumped on me. All that was left was the Y, and "why" wasn't easy to answer. Sure, I could blame it all on Tony, but that was only part of it. Why had I let myself be treated that way? Why hadn't I known better? Maybe I wasn't as perceptive as I thought when it came to judging people. My track record lately hadn't been too good.

I went back into the living room. "Alec," I called to him. "I want to talk to you." He came out of the kitchen.

"Now what? Was it something I said or something I did?"

"It's nothing like that. I want to know everything — what Tony was up to. What he was doing, what he was telling people, what you meant by that comment you made."

"Haven't you forgotten Tony?"

"Yeah, I have. More or less. But I can't put him behind me till I know everything."

"We've been through this before. Why don't we just go to bed?"

"You brought him up."

"You're going to get mad at me."

"I won't. I promise."

"What do you want to know?"

"For starters, how come so many people knew Tony?"

"He'd been around a long time. Since before you ever came to town."

"Go on."

"Oh, shit! Tony had sex with half the guys in town. They used to call him Tony the Tunnel. They say he could take two men at once."

"Anyone I know?"

"You don't know many people. All right, don't give me that look. Everyone you know."

"Including you?"

"Joe. . . ."

"Look — my hand is steady. I'm perfectly calm. Tell me."

"Yes, me, too. And Tom and Randy, before they got together, and I suppose even Harold and God knows who else. There was this party once, it turned into a real orgy."

My stomach turned over at the thought — Harold and Tony? If anything good had happened to me all week, it was that I hadn't had much to eat that night so I only felt slightly sick. Tony the Tunnel and Professor Barf. They deserved each other. I swallowed a couple of times. "Why do people think Tony and I broke up?"

"He said he was tired of you, that you were smothering him, holding him back from making it big in the city. That's what he told people."

"When? Who? He didn't talk to the bar crowd any more."

"For cryin' out loud, Joe, are you blind and deaf, or just dumb? Do you think Tony was a faithful little lapdog all the time you were together? People still saw him. In the Alamo, the tea room."

"The tea room? On campus?"

"Tony was as big a whore after you met him as he was before. I can't believe you didn't know."

"How could I know? He kept me at home away from other people, fed me this crap about how we shouldn't mingle with the riff raff. How we should be exclusive! I was flattered, thought he was jealous over the possibility of me meeting other people, when all the time he was really trying to keep me from finding out the truth about him, the shit! That fucking shit!"

"So that's why you were such a snob. He really had you going, didn't he? Kept his blond mystery man hidden away while he catted around on the side."

"What did you call me?"

"Call you? His blond mystery man?"

"Why'd you say that?"

"I, uh, no reason."

"Alec!"

"For God's sake, do you think people don't know where you two met? Everyone knew you were a tea room queen. You don't think you can keep it a secret just by trying to hide your face, do you? That makes people talk even more. One day you're wiping that toilet floor with your ass, and the next day you're running around with Tony the Tunnel acting like you're the Queen of Sheba. And you wonder why nobody wants to meet you!"

I felt like the world's biggest dope. How dumb can a guy get? Me and my secret life, my discretion. My perfect relationship with that bastard Tony. Thanks to him I was the village idiot. I'd never be able to show my face in public again!

"Joe, you're not mad at me, are you?"

"No. Just at myself."

"Joe, I know you're not stupid, but you've got to be the most naive person I've ever met. You strut your stuff like you're Mr. Universe, but you're really just a big innocent, inexperienced kid. I suppose that's why I like you."

"I must be the laughing stock of the whole town."

"Not the whole town, just the 20 percent of the population, give or take a few percentage points, that's gay."

"Thanks a lot." I knew he was trying to make light of it, but I wasn't in the mood for laughing.

"Oh, come on, Joe, it's not that bad."

"No? With the opinion people have of me, I'm surprised that *you* even talk to me."

"That's what I'm here for." He smiled and started to sing. " 'Ya got me, baby, ya got me.' "

I managed to smile back. I said good night and got into bed knowing I wouldn't sleep a wink all night. I just tossed and turned, getting madder and madder. I'd never be able to face anyone again. Not the bar crowd, the Birdies, Harold — all those people I always felt superior to. And what about Rob? My one glimmer of hope was that maybe he hadn't heard all about me. OK, so he hung around with Tom and Randy, but he admitted he wasn't all that crazy about them, didn't want to listen to their gossip. That's what I needed, someone shy and reserved, who didn't say much, who kept his distance and smiled that smile. But what was the point of hoping? What could I do, hang around the Alamo in the hope he'd come in? Ask Tom and Randy to fix me up? I might as well forget Rob. I was finished in this town.

By morning I'd resolved to pack up and leave. But where would I go? Back home to the farm, to listen to grandma explain to me about the tricks life plays? Well, I'd seen enough of life to tell her a thing or two. I could tell them all a thing or two, all those narrow-minded rednecks who made my life hell and then carried on like I'd died when I said I wanted to leave home, to see more of the world than cornstalks and hay. I'd seen it, all right. I'd seen plenty. And heard even more. I didn't belong on the farm any more. But I didn't belong here, either. Life is like shit. The deeper you step in it, the worse it stinks. What do you think of those words of wisdom, eh, grandma?

At least in the apartment I felt safe. Alec would take care of me, he understood me. And he was all I had.

ACT TWO

SCENE I

Best Foot Forward

You're supposed to feel better in the morning. There were enough songs about that — the sun'll come out, right? The sun *was* out, its reflection hitting my tired eyes as it bounced off the glass-covered posters in the living room. Those shows Alec loved so much. By this time I knew them well enough to know that in *Hallelujah, Baby!* they sang about how tomorrow was another day. And in *Dear World,* didn't Angela Lansbury say that tomorrow morning you could begin again? God, I felt like hell and here I was doing medleys.

I was so tired I skipped my workout — it was all I could do to drag myself to the store. And that meant seeing Judy. I did my best to stay away from her, keeping one of the other guys between her and me, rushing up to help every customer who came in. But I could feel her watching me. If I glanced her way, she'd smile or wink, and once, when I couldn't avoid passing by her, she whispered, "Don't worry, Joe, I'm not gonna bite you. Yet." Which almost made me laugh — it sounded like a line from *Superman.* Like Alec always said, everything is a song cue.

After a day or two, Judy was more or less under control. I only had to put up with occasional reports on how she'd lost another pound or moved up a weight on some machine at the gym. I changed my own schedule at the club, going in a little later to avoid both Judy and Jerry. But the place was dead between the morning rush and the lunch-hour crowd, so my heart wasn't really in it. My heart wasn't anyplace. My life was a dull routine, no changes, no choices, nothing to look forward to. I discovered I'd been doing eighteen repetitions on the tricep machine without even thinking to increase the weight. Even running had become a drag. I changed my route in order to pass a big construction site, but it was still too cold for the workers to go shirtless. And at night, I just sat around the apartment waiting for Alec to get home from those rehearsals. With the opening of the play so close, he was putting in more and more time at the theater and always coming home real hyper, especially if Kelly had said something nice to him. I'd just sit there looking gloomy, maybe sigh now and then to get his attention. I kept hoping he'd want to console me with cookies or some little treat he'd put away. He was too damn busy to even bake!

It took a few days, but Alec finally did notice my rotten mood. I could tell by the songs he sang. "Climb Ev'ry Mountain" was not his usual kind of tune for cooking breakfast to, and "You Mustn't Be Discouraged" wasn't appropriate for washing dishes, even if he was imitating Carol Burnett imitating Shirley Temple. By the time he'd run through "Hey, Look Me Over," "High Is Better Than Low," and "I Ain't Down Yet," I knew he was trying to tell me to pull myself together. After his spirited rendition of "There's Gotta Be Something Better Than This" with a staccato accompaniment of stomping feet, I'd had enough.

"OK, Alec, I get the message. You can quit now."

"Thank God," he said. "I can't do that last number justice without spiked heels, and my feet are killing me as it is."

"I appreciate the effort, but it's going to take more than a song to cheer me up."

"Snap out of it, Joe, things can't be that bad."

"Easy for you to say. I've hit rock bottom. I can't face people, not after the way I behaved all those months with Tony, especially not after the things he must have been saying about me all over town. No one will every want to meet me. What am I going to do?"

"I'm hardly in a position to give advice. I've let that show take over my life. Once it opens, I'll be right back where I was. The same old routine."

"Yeah, but you've got Kelly."

"Sure, as long as I'm useful to him. After the show I'll probably never see him again."

"Why would you think that?"

"Look, he's an important guy — a professor, an experienced director — just the other day I found out he's spent time in New York, even did a play off-Broadway. Why should he be interested in someone like me?"

"Here we go again. Why *shouldn't* he be interested? You've got a lot to offer."

"Like for instance?"

"Let's see. You're smart, witty. A great cook. And nice looking."

"I sound too good to be true."

"If you'd stop putting yourself down. Could we get back to the subject? We're supposed to be solving my problem, not yours."

"You're perfect. We both know that."

"No I'm not. If I was perfect I wouldn't be in this predicament. I have to change. And you have to help me."

"I'm supposed to help you change? That's a laugh. Where should we start? Your singing? Dancing? Your dress size?"

"That's *not* what I mean. I have to learn how to meet people, how to talk to them. So they'll realize I'm not as stuck-up as everyone thinks. We have to make me more. . . likable. So guys will want to know me."

"Ah, a makeover. Now *that* might be fun. Like in *Illya Darling,* when Homer tries to educate Melina Mercouri — she's Illya — teach her to appreciate the finer things in life."

"What happens?"

"She ends up one hell of an unhappy hooker." He laughed. "No, that doesn't sound like it's going to help. Let's see, Mame tries to make over Agnes Gooch. But she comes back pregnant." We both laughed. "Of course, the classic makeover is *My Fair Lady.*"

"But that one's different. Don't they fall in love, at the end?"

"After a fashion. Though I doubt Professor Higgins would ever admit as much. He only goes so far as to say he's gotten accustomed to her. I guess you take what you can get." He glanced over at me and seemed to give me a quick once-over. "No, I suppose I'm the one who'd need the makeover before anything like that ever happened."

"Anything like what?"

"Nothing." He sighed. "You know, this might be instructive, making me over. Come on, Joe, tell me what you'd change about me."

"What do you mean?"

"Just pretend you were comparing me to your ideal man. Theoretically speaking. I'd need muscles, right?" He curled his fist and pressed against his biceps with his thumb. "What do you think? Would muscle do it?"

"A little muscle never hurt anyone. But you'd look pretty funny when you were in drag. You'd have to give that up."

"Oh, I don't know. The padded shoulder look has a certain timeless elegance. Wouldn't it be fun if we could wear the same clothes?"

"Mine or yours?"

He laughed. "Come on, this is getting interesting. What else would you change about me?" I didn't know what his point was, so I just shrugged. "Joe, you're not entering into this at all. We've ruled out drag, ruled in muscles. Let's see, I suppose singing would have to go, unless I cultivated a bass voice. Dance numbers would definitely be out. And I'd have to cut myself off from all my friends, wouldn't I?"

"Alec, I don't know what you're talking about. Why would I want you any different?"

He rolled his eyes and threw up his hands. "Why would you want me at all? I don't know why I do this to myself. Forget the whole thing."

"*What* whole thing?"

Suddenly he seemed annoyed. "Joe, sometimes you're so. . .so. . .obtuse! Just leave me alone, OK? He went to his room and closed the door.

I knew he'd been edgy lately. I figured it had to do with Kelly and the play. I didn't want to make things any harder for him, but he seemed to be upset with me and I hadn't a clue as to why he was acting so strange. I knocked on his door. "Alec?" He didn't answer, so I pushed the door open. He was lying on the bed. "Are you OK?"

He sat up. "Don't pay any attention to me. I've been a little nervous lately."

"Look, if there's something bothering you, something I've done. . . ."

He looked at me kind of suspiciously, like he couldn't decide whether or not to say what he was thinking. "Why are you still living here, Joe? Half the time we argue, the other half you stay in your room to avoid my friends. I mean, do you and I have *anything* in common?"

I felt kind of defensive. What was he trying to do, throw me out? I knew I had to come up with something. "Well, we both like to eat."

He shook his head and started to laugh. "Whoever

said the way to a man's heart is through his stomach had no idea what I'm up against here."

He was losing me again. "Come on, Alec, we get along OK. Most of the time."

"If you say so." He sat on the edge of the bed. "Now where were we?"

"You were going to help me, you know, kind of overcome my past."

"Forget about the past. Meet new people. Go back to school. There are a lot of new faces in the summer."

"School?"

"Well, you say you're going to finish. Why not now?"

"Who wants to spend the summer reading and studying? That's not what summer's for."

"What *is* it for? Don't tell me, it's for wearing those little blue running shorts and showing yourself off all over town."

"Hey, a guy has to have a tan, doesn't he? I mean, you wouldn't want me to be all pale and sick-looking, would you?"

He held out his hands and glanced at his arms. "Perish the thought. It's nice to know we have your summer plans worked out."

"I think you're making fun of me. I feel it's important that a guy look his best. What's wrong with that?"

"Joe, you'd look good no matter what color you were. You're a great looking guy. Maybe you're *too* attractive. Ordinary guys are afraid of approaching someone like you. Especially someplace like the bar, where everyone's watching. That's why you've got to take it slow, get to know people, let things happen at their own pace. But you can't sit around feeling sorry for yourself. Get out, do things. Like the play — there's going to be a party afterwards. Come with me. There'll be all sorts of people there."

"A party? The play?"

"You're going, aren't you? You don't mean to tell me that after all these weeks of hearing nothing in this apartment except that damned play, you're not going?"

"I don't have a ticket."

"Take mine. I won't be sitting down. I'll be all over the theater helping Kelly keep track of everything, telling Harold whether he's liking it or not. You'll enjoy it, if you let yourself."

"I'll think about it."

"You *have* to go. So you can go to the party. And sweep some lucky guy off his feet. Besides, if you don't, I won't give you any peace. For starters, there's 'Come Along with Me,' 'Follow Me,' 'Come A-Wandering with Me,'. . ."

"OK, OK, since you put it that way."

"In the words of the immortal Merm, 'To the hunt!' "

SCENE II

The Roar of the Greasepaint

By the time Alec had treated me to several day's worth of songs about determination, I began to think things might not be so bad after all. What Alec had told me, really, was just to be myself, and he made it clear that myself was damned good-looking, so why shouldn't I be able to meet someone? And if I had to go to that play, and the party, to prove it to myself, I would. Alec would know everyone there. He'd introduce me around, help me break the ice. I could always count on Alec when I needed him.

The day of the opening he treated me to a non-stop medley of theater tunes: "There's No Business Like Show Business," "Another Op'nin', Another Show," "Be a Performer," "Welcome to the Theater." It was only after dinner, when he gave me my ticket and left early, that I realized I was finally on my own.

I hate going to things myself. I feel conspicuous, like everyone is thinking, poor guy, has no friends. What really hurt was that it was true! So I got to the theater just a few minutes before the play was scheduled to start, took my seat, and pretended to be fascinated by the program. There was a girl on my right holding hands with her date, and the seat on the left was empty. I half expected to see Harold park himself in it and start drooling all over me. The lights were already dimming before someone sat down. I glanced over. It was Rob, cheekbones and all.

"Hi," he said, nodding. "How's it going?" I was so surprised I didn't answer. I hardly heard the overture. All I could think about was that he'd spoken to me and I hadn't said anything. I was furious with myself.

The show turned out to be pretty good. I didn't even mind the drag role. You weren't supposed to know that it was a guy till the end, but I'm a keen observer of people, and besides, I recognized the guy from the Alamo. Captain Hook, Alec said they called him.

I'd heard *Chicago* a hundred times in the last few weeks, so the songs were familir, and this show — well, it was definitely no *Sound of Music.* In fact, I was kind of surprised. This play was really *about* something, not just an icky love story like I thought all those musicals were. This one had something to say. And it was a lot more exciting seeing it live up there, not just hearing a record; I was able to understand why Alec liked these musicals so much. I wouldn't think twice about seeing another one.

I spotted the Birdies in the chorus; they had a few different parts each — policemen, reporters. They weren't bad. At least they didn't flutter all over the stage. They could act like men, when they were acting.

At the intermission I was afraid Rob would leave before I could think of something to say. But he spoke first, asked me what I thought of the show.

"I like it. How come you're not in it?"

"I'm the choreographer." He opened his program and pointed to his name. Robert Welch. A good, solid name. I was afraid it might be something like, you know, Robin LaRue.

"So that's you, huh?"

'That's me.''

''Well, the dancing's good. I liked the opening number.''

He flicked his hair back, the same gesture I'd noticed when I first spotted him in the bar. He'd seemed arrogant then. But I supposed that if I had fine soft brown hair that fell across my forehead in a way that no doubt made half the people I met want to comb it back with their fingers, I'd probably flick it in place myself. ''Thanks,'' he said, matter of factly, ''I did what I could with what I had. Are you going out to the lobby? I've got to mingle. People expect it.''

I followed him up the aisle. If I tagged along, I could act like I was with him; it was better than being alone. And if he didn't mingle too much, we could talk, maybe get a conversation going that we'd want to finish later at the party. Now I had a good reason to go.

We spotted Harold in the middle of the crowd, waving his arms and making sure everyone knew he was there. ''It's marvelous, isn't it? Of course there are rough spots, opening night jitters, I'm sure, but for a group of *kids,* I'm *impressed.* Oh, there's our choreographer. Rob, oh Rob, come here! I *must* tell you how much I'm enjoying it.''

Rob smirked, and I hoped he'd ignore Harold's call. But he lifted his head, forced his mouth into a smile and flicked his hair. *''Noblesse oblige,''* he said to me before he set off toward Harold.

So much for our talk. I went to the john and started back through the lobby to my seat. Alec spotted me and made his way over. ''Having a good time?'' he asked me.

''Yeah, it's OK. Rob has the seat next to me. He had to go talk to Harold.''

''I've already had that pleasure.''

''So how are you getting along with Kelly?''

He shrugged. ''It's been too hectic. He's all nerves. I'm hoping we can talk later, at the party. I'll try to go with him.

Ask Rob for the address; he can tell you how to get there, it's just across campus."

The lights flashed and I took my seat. Rob barely made it before the music started. When the show ended, I took a deep breath and asked him if he knew where the party was going to be. He offered me a lift. Things were getting off to a good start. Maybe this party was going to be fun after all.

It seemed like a good start, at least till I learned we had to wait for the Birdies to change out of their costumes. On the drive over, I had to listen to them carry on.

"I thought it went great. Didn't it go great?"

"Pretty good."

"Pretty good? It was great. What wasn't great?"

"Andrea wasn't really on."

"Andrea was great. Paul was nervous."

"Paul was fine. Rob, wasn't Paul fine?"

"Everyone was fine."

This went on for fifteen minutes. No one even asked what I thought. It was like I wasn't even there. Not that I cared, but I was sitting in the front seat, right next to Rob. Someone might have at least asked. I hoped the drive wasn't going to be a preview of the rest of the night. I didn't know what to expect — I had no idea who was giving the party or who would be there. Probably all theater types. I'd have a hard time getting Rob to myself. And I wanted to, badly. Here was a guy who, if he knew anything about me, wasn't letting it stand in his way, a guy who spoke to me, offered me a lift, actually seemed to want my company. I was anxious to find out what was going on behind those cheekbones.

The party was in a fancy high-rise apartment in the part of town where faculty members lived. The host was a middle-aged piss-elegant queen who said "theatuh" and was "charmed" to meet me. But the food was good, the drinks generous. The guests were a mix of young and old, more men than women, some outrageous people of both sexes. Not the sort I was comfortable with. I wanted to stay close to Rob, but he was swallowed up in the crowd. So I got a drink and stood in a corner behind a big plant and wondered what I'd gotten myself into.

"Are you an actor?"

I looked around and saw this guy about sixty. Silver hair, expensive clothes, a scarf knotted around his neck. "No."

"Well, how did you get here?"

"Rob brought me."

"Ah, Rob. Figures."

"What figures?"

"That he'd be the one to uncover a specimen like you. Quite lovely. I didn't know Rob had anything going."

I hated the way people jumped to conclusions. "I hardly know him."

"Just picked you up along the side of the road, I suppose. You had your. . .thumb. . .sticking out. Are those muscles real?"

"Look, he didn't pick me up anywhere. I've known him a while. He's a friend of a friend."

"Indeed. Would you like to be an actor?"

"Me?"

"I'm not talking to the *ficus,* dear. What a face! What a build! I can assure you, you've got what it takes."

"I thought it took talent."

He smiled at me. "There's talent and there's talent. A good director can always find what there is to work with."

"Thanks, but I'm not interested."

"I'm George Willard. I run the Downtown Players, you know, on Court Street? I could help you. Would you like to come see me?"

The branches of the plant shook, and we both turned. "Does George have you auditioning yet?" Rob asked.

The guy waved his hand. ''Keep it in mind. What was your name?''

''I'll keep it in mind.''

''He never stops trying,'' Rob said, shaking his head.

I shrugged. ''It's not every day someone offers to make me a star. Maybe I should be flattered.''

''I shouldn't think so. If George *didn't* come on to you, then you might have something to worry about.'' He looked around the room. ''You can't trust anyone. Especially a guy like him — put a little fish in a small enough pond, it'll start thinking it's big.''

This George Willard hadn't struck me as anything more than a guy on the make, and I could hardly blame him for that. But I guess Rob knew him a lot better than I did, so I figured I should probably be grateful to him for setting me straight. ''I wasn't expecting such dangerous people.'' I said, hoping a smile would get one in return. ''I may need help keeping the sharks away.''

''I wouldn't worry if I were you,'' he said, with a tired look. ''The water here is pretty shallow.''

Just then there was a big commotion at the door. We both turned to see Harold arriving with an entourage of cast members. ''Oh, shit,'' Rob muttered, flicking back his hair. ''Here we go again. See you later.''

He left me in my corner, wondering what to make of him. I supposed it was hard having to play all the games these people played, and I could sympathize with anyone who was forced to be nice to Harold. Rob must have been under a lot of pressure that night.

Alec arrived with Harold and found me a few minutes later. ''Was that Rob you were talking to? You two are getting pretty chummy.''

''This is hardly the place to get to know someone. Where's Kelly?''

''He didn't come. Said he had too much on his mind.''

"Too bad."

"I guess. I think this would be a good time for me to start forgetting about him. Are you ready for a refill? I need a drink."

I followed him across the living room. Several people stopped to talk to him, but he clearly wasn't in the mood for conversation. Some music started and the crowd backed up to make room for dancing. We got our drinks and stopped to watch. After a few minutes, the dancing couples moved aside, and I could see that Rob had become the center of attention. I'd never seen anyone move the way he did, like he was rubber instead of bones, graceful, smooth, absolutely beautiful.

"He's good, isn't he?" Alec whispered in my ear. I just nodded, thinking to myself that a Portuguese longshoreman's shirt and South African miner's pants had never looked better.

The circle widened and the Birdies moved onto the dance floor. At first Rob seemed not to notice, but then he smiled and the three of them were dancing with each other. Tom and Randy took turns approaching Rob with sexy, suggestive moves, and he responded in kind. The crowd was whooping and clapping. The night was ruined for me. When Alec said he was going to leave, I decided to go with him. I wasn't in a party mood any more, either. I turned back for a last look at the dancers. Rob was lost in his own world. He wouldn't miss me.

It took us a good half hour to walk home, but neither of us said much. We both had our minds on other things. We felt tired and let down when we got in the door, so we said good night. As I started getting undressed, I felt the program I'd shoved into my back pocket. I pulled it out and took another look at it. "Choreography by Robert Welch." So he could dance. Why did he have to make a spectacle of himself with the Birdies? In front of all those people? I folded up the program and was about to toss it when my eye caught something on the back.

"Hey, Alec?"

"What is it?"

"Come here. Quick"

He came running in, his pants undone, his shirt open. It was the first time I'd seen him even partly undressed. I'd never realized he had hair on his chest. I'd always just assumed, to the extent that I ever thought about it, that he'd be hairless and scrawny, like a plucked chicken. But the hair was dark and thick, with a fine line down to his navel. I forgot myself for an instant. I always like a hairy chest on a guy.

"Well, say something, Joe. What's the big deal?"

"Oh, this." I held out the program. "Have you taken a good look?" He shook his head. "There, on the back."

He glanced at it. "What?"

"Alec! Where it says 'acknowledgments.' See where the director thanks a whole bunch of people. Under that. 'With very special thanks' — I think you'll find your name! That ought to cheer you up."

He looked at me and smiled. "You know, Joe, you're really very sweet."

"Is that all you can say? What about Kelly singling you out like that?"

"He didn't."

"What do you mean? It says, right there —"

"I wrote it. They were late getting it to the printer, so Kelly asked me to help out. Gave me that list of names. I was pissed that he hadn't included me, so I added that. Thought it might shake him up. Get him to think about all the help I've given him. I doubt he's even seen it."

"Alec, you're impossible."

"Well, it was a good try. But I really appreciate your

wanting to make me feel better.'' He moved toward me like he wanted to hug me, then pulled back.

''Something wrong?'' I asked him.

''I just didn't want you to think I was 'getting any ideas.' ''

I couldn't help but laugh. Then I grabbed his skinny body and gave him his hug. I could feel the hair on his chest scratching against my shirt and see where those little swirls on the back of his neck disappeared down his collar. What the hell, I thought, it'd been a long time. So I hugged him tighter. Funny thing, though. He didn't feel as skinny as he looked.

SCENE III

Seesaw

Alec wasn't in a very good mood the rest of the weekend. It was only natural that he'd feel let down after all the weeks he'd put in on the show, but he convinced himself that he didn't stand a chance with Kelly. " 'Thank you for such a little but lovely time,' " he sang as he cooked our Sunday breakfast, and whenever he mentioned Kelly's name, he preceded it with "bastard" or "ingrate." But we did have a good laugh over Harold's review of the play. Alec had dictated most of it to him on their way to the party, but Harold had felt the need to add a few thoughts of his own. It ended up an odd mixture of serious comments and foolish gushes, a regular barf paper.

I couldn't decide what kind of mood I was in. I kept trying to make up my mind about Rob. He'd talked to me in the theater, sought me out afterward at the party. Why would he have bothered unless he was interested in me? But how could he have danced like that with the Birdies? Dancing with one other man was bad enough, in front of an audience, but with two others? Then again, he *was* a dancer, a performer. He was probably used to doing things in front of people. And God knows, he was attractive. OK, so he did seem a little sharp-tongued, but who could blame him, with all those creepy theater-type people at the party? For once, I vowed, I wasn't going to be too quick to judge. I'd do like Alec said, let things go at their own pace. We'd just have to get to know each other.

By Sunday night Alec and I had spent most of our day sitting across from each other while we read the paper, shifting our positions, not being able to get comfortable, staring off into space while we tried to sort out our thoughts.

"This is useless," Alec moaned, throwing the paper aside. He got up and came back with the brandy. He handed me a glass and settled into his chair. "It has not been the best weekend of my life," he sighed.

"Don't be so pessimistic. That guy Kelly will learn to appreciate you. That is, if he has any brains."

"Thanks." He looked at me and smiled. "I guess that party didn't turn out to be much fun for you, either."

"In a way it did."

"How so?"

"Rob. I think he's interested in me."

"Rob? Do you like *him*?"

"Well, I don't really know him. At least not yet. You seem surprised. Don't you think he's worth a try?"

"He, uh, just doesn't strike me as your type. I mean, he's friends with Tom and Randy. That should be the kiss of death right there."

"He's different. Not like them."

"If you say so. Still, he's a theater person, and you hate theater people, all us fluttery, effeminate types."

"Oh, Alec, you're OK."

"Am I? You didn't used to think so."

"You're not like you used to be. You've changed."

"No, I haven't changed. Maybe you have."

"Me? Why would you say that?"

He shrugged. "I guess you've gotten used to me. And all my bad habits. And my friends. And *their* friends."

"I don't know why you're bringing all this up. It almost sounds like you're looking for a fight."

"Well, maybe I am," he said in an angry tone of voice. "I'd just like to know why the hell you'd suddenly be taken with someone like Rob. You can't stand Tom and Randy, you'd think I was contaminated for hanging around with them, so now you go and get hung up on one of their other friends."

"I'd've thought you'd be glad. Sure, there are things about him I don't like. In fact, what it comes down to *is* Tom and Randy, the way he carries on with those two flitty friends of yours. But I'm trying to overlook that. Maybe it's a good sign, you know, like I've become more open-minded or something. Besides, he seems to be pursuing me."

"Is that all it takes? Someone just has to show a little interest?"

"If that's all it took, I'd be married to Harold by now. I don't know why you're riding me like this. Rob is awfully attractive, and he has a fantastic build."

He stood up and shouted at me. "God damn it, Joe, is that all that's important to you? That a guy has a good build?"

"What's the matter with you, Alec? You're jumping down my throat no matter what I say. For cryin' out loud, I met the guy right here, at one of your stupid parties. What's gotten into you?"

He sat down and put his face in his hands. "You're right," he said, shaking his head. "Rob is good-looking, I can't deny that. And if that's what you want . . . . I ought to know better by now." He sipped his brandy and seemed to calm down. "You like Rob? Fine. Good luck. I'll invite him to our Tony Award party next month. See how you like his costume."

"Does that mean it's dress-up time again?"

"And how! Of course, we need a theme. It's getting harder, what with the state the theater is in. Any ideas? I hear you're a lot more open-minded these days."

Now he was getting me mad. ''It would never be my idea to pretend I was a girl. I wish you could explain to me how you can do that.''

''It's just for fun. It's silly. Don't you ever do anything silly?''

''Not that.''

''What *do* you do for fun? Pose in front of the mirror in those little blue shorts?''

''You seem to have a fixation on those running shorts. Don't tell me even the great, noble Alec admires a good-looking guy when he sees one.''

''Touche,'' he said, with a raised eyebrow. ''The man knows how to twist the knife.''

''And you know how to change the subject. Whatever I do, it's not the same as dressing up in women's clothes. Is that what you want, to be a girl? Is that why you always put yourself down?''

''I rather like myself, most of the time. It's other people that depress me.''

''So you sing songs instead of living real life. That's not normal.''

''Ah, but that's where you're wrong. We all have our masks, we all hide behind something. Your macho routine is no different from my flamboyant behavior. It's a cover-up.''

''Oh yeah? For what?''

He shrugged. ''For that part of you that wants to. . .who knows, do window displays.''

''That wasn't my idea.''

''I know, forced on you by a cruel, hostile world. You tell me, then, Joe. Why are you so hung up on acting butch? Why are my friends and I so threatening?''

''Threatening? That's a laugh. How could those clowns threaten me?''

''Then why don't you like them? Afraid of a little mascara rubbing off on you?''

"I told you. They're stereotypes. They give us all a bad name. God knows it's hard enough being gay without guys like them running loose."

"You should be grateful to them — they make it easier for guys like you to hide. Because that's all you're doing, hiding behind your muscles."

"It's better than hiding behind a dress."

"Have it your way. What difference does it make? We all have our hangups."

I could have let it drop then. Maybe I should have. He seemed ready to call it quits. But he'd started this fight, and I wasn't about to let him off the hook. "All right, Alec. You're always so ready to analyze me — what are your 'hangups'?"

He stared into his glass, then leaned his head back. The fight seemed to drain out of him. He was ignoring my question, avoiding a serious talk, like he always did. But then he smiled to himself.

"Is something funny?"

"I was just thinking," he said, shaking his head. "About when I was a kid. And Burt, the town bully. He sure made my life hell. Him and most of the other boys I went to school with. But Burt, I'd go ten blocks out of my way to avoid him. My only escape was make-believe. I know, lots of kids dream of being performers. Except the others, they'd try to pick out the guitar chords to the top forty hits. They wanted to be *like* someone else; not me, I wanted to *be* someone else, someone far away — in Siam, Oklahoma, Bali Ha'i. I pestered my parents for lessons, piano, singing, dancing. I was a regular one-man show. Then it was time for my first recital. I was all done up in red, white, and blue for this snappy tap routine. "Yankee Doodle Dandy." But I peeked out from behind the curtain, and you know who I saw in the front row? Big old Burt, there to watch his sister. I couldn't move. So they sent out the next kid, and the next, and the next, and at the end, I heard the applause for everyone else, everyone but me. Something snapped. I knew I'd never hear it for me. I didn't have what it takes to face the bullies. Not then, not now. To this day I can't even listen to a song by George M. Cohan."

"Your folks must have been furious. What'd they do?"

"My folks? Oh, they were great. Took me out for ice cream, told me I could sing just for them. But I realized the futility of it all. I quit the lessons. Now I take what I know and sell a lot of records and see to it Harold doesn't fall on his ass. But in my own apartment, I'm the biggest star there is."

"I'm sorry, I never realized . . . . At least your parents were understanding. Mine would've killed me. I mean, they wouldn't have even let me *talk* to a guy who took dance lessons. I had to be the perfect little man. And if I wasn't . . . . I can still feel that hairbrush on my behind."

"That's too bad, Joe. Maybe it's why you're so uptight about so many things."

"Maybe. Where I come from, the only thing that's ever 'gay' is the new dress someone's maiden aunt is going to wear to the church social. I try to picture Harold coming on the TV in my hometown. I can just see those farmers rubbing their chins and wondering whose field the Martians had landed in."

"I can imagine." He laughed. "But at least there's one good thing."

"What's that?"

"Your behind didn't suffer any permanent damage?"

"Oh, Alec. You really *are* impossible."

So we were friends again. Still, all I could think of when I got into bed that night was how weird Alec had been acting lately. I thought he'd be pleased when I told him I had my eye on Rob. Wasn't I doing what he suggested, going out to that party, getting to know someone new? But instead of being glad, he seemed annoyed, almost as if he was jealous. But that wasn't possible. You had to be in love with someone in order to be jealous. I mean, we argued half the time, he said so himself. I'll say this about Alec, he could make me madder than anyone ever did before, except Tony, of course, and what I felt for Tony, if it wasn't love, I at least thought it was. But Alec, he'd been pretty mad, too. I could tell — he hadn't sung a single song all night. Whatever was eating him, it must have been because of Kelly. The guy would have to be a real dope not to have liked Alec. But even if Kelly *was* the cause of Alec's strange behavior, that didn't explain why I was feeling so confused.

In any case, I was glad Alec and I had our talk. I understood him better, saw why he was the person he was. He hadn't turned out all that bad, considering the suffering he must have gone through. I could only imagine how painful that had been. Like grandma used to say, you have to sleep in another man's long-johns to know where he itches the most.

SCENE IV

My One and Only

The play was scheduled to run again the following weekend. In the meantime, Alec decided to stay away from the theater in the hope that Kelly would miss him at the extra rehearsals he'd called. It had been a long time since Alec had been home in the evenings, and we fell back into our old routine. We'd have a nice dinner, a snack if I'd worked late; we'd fill each other in on the day's events, maybe listen to a record. If Alec couldn't decide what he wanted to hear, I'd look through his albums and help him make up his mind. The time I spent at home was a welcome relief from the rest of my dreary life.

Jerry nailed me one day at the gym after I was buckled into the super lower back machine and tried to arrange another breakfast. I managed to put him off, but all that talk made me miss my count and do extra reps, and I hate that machine most of all. Later that same day, Judy cornered me in the back room at the store to give me a diet update and let me know she was ready for me whenever I said the word.

"I'm not good enough for you, Judy," I told her.

"Don't worry," she winked. "I'll bet you're good enough."

Ralph, the store wise-guy, saw us huddling and

asked me if I'd heard the one about the guy who stuck his finger in the dyke.

"If he pulled out his thumb and called it sheep-dip," I muttered, "I don't want to hear about it." He looked at me like I was crazy. But what I was, was fed up. "And besides, Ralph, what makes you such an expert on people, huh? If I were you, I wouldn't be so damn quick to judge someone on the basis of her looks."

His mouth fell open and he stood there staring at me. For once he didn't have some smart-ass comment. But he'd had it coming. I mean, Ralph was the one who put it in my head in the first place that Judy must be gay. And I fell for it because I was so damn uptight about what he might start saying about *me.* That was my whole trouble, wasn't it? Letting myself be led down the garden path by the likes of Ralph. And Jerry. And Tony. Well, I'd had it! I didn't care that Ralph was still giving me funny looks an hour later. I supposed that meant it would be all over the store that Judy and I were an item. Let them talk. It was the closest thing to a relationship I had going!

I'd decided to follow Alec's lead and wait till the show had ended its run before I tried to see Rob. He'd be more relaxed, then, more mellow. But in the meantime, I was feeling antsy. So antsy that I decided to pay a visit to the campus tea room. The last trace of that welt was gone, and I'd started being real careful not to let the straps of the Nautilus machines leave any marks or bruises. Just my luck, the place was a mess. They were tearing out a wall to provide access to the building's elevator, and two stalls had been combined to provide railings for the handicapped. "Tap toe for action" just didn't seem appropriate any more. It was the end of an era. The blond mystery man retreated and beat himself off at home. Some things never changed.

''Well, Alec,'' I began one morning the following week, ''the play is over. We can resume our pursuit of Rob and Kelly.''

''You do what you want. I've given up.''

''You can't give up! I thought we were in this together.''

''It's not a contest, you know.''

''I know. I just don't want to see you end up alone.''

''That's very sweet of you. Really. But don't worry about me. I don't want to hold you back.''

''But I was counting on you to help me. I don't know what to do next.''

He shrugged. ''Take the bull by the horns. Go see him. He's a teaching assistant this year, he must have an office. Probably in the Fine Arts building, near Harold and Kelly.''

''I can't just drop in. That's exactly the sort of thing I'm no good at. I need a reason to be on campus.''

''Joe, I can't do everything for you. You're the one who's hot for the guy — find a reason.''

''Come on, Alec, I'm new at this. You have to help. What can I do?''

He sighed. ''How should I know? Say you're there to pick up a summer school schedule. Ask Rob to suggest a course.''

''Summer school?''

''Look, I didn't say you had to register for classes, but it would give you an excuse for going up there.''

''I guess, Alec?''

''Now what?''

''I don't know where the Fine Arts building is.''

He threw up his hands. "All right. I give up, I'll go with you. But only till we find Rob's office. Then I'll go see Harold."

"Or Kelly."

"Who ever thought I'd end up with Dolly Levi on my hands? You're a regular Yenta the matchmaker."

"I'm just trying to help."

"I know, I know." He pushed me out the door.

Twenty minutes later we were in the lobby of the Fine Arts building. Alec helped me find Rob's office number, and we headed for the elevator.

"Aren't you forgetting something?" he asked.

"What do you mean?"

"There's a pile of catalogs over there. You'll need a prop."

I went back for a course list and caught the next elevator. I was feeling a little nervous, almost hoped Rob wouldn't be there. But I kept reminding myself that he was the one who started the conversations at the play and the party afterwards. And besides, I'd caught a little sun on my last few runs, so I looked especially good.

He was sitting behind the desk, talking to a student. The thought of having to wait made me even more jittery, so I sat down on the floor and started thumbing through the course list. I remembered how much fun that had always seemed, when I was in school, the start of a new session. I'd read all the descriptions, thinking how exciting the classes sounded, wonder what the prof would be like, who would be in the course. Every semester I'd vow to stay up on the work so I wouldn't have to cram at the end, then I'd end up cramming anyway. Even that was fun, in a way, hanging around the library with all the other students who'd let it slide all semester. I missed school, sort of. But if I took one class during each of the two summer sessions, I'd get a good start on making up the credits I lost when I quit.

"Joe?" I looked up, startled. I'd almost forgotten why I was there. Rob had walked the student to the door and was looking down at me, his hair falling over his forehead. He looked great in a Greek dockworker's shirt and Italian army pants, with real titanium buttons. Not to mention his Punjab sandals. And from this angle, he was all cheekbones.

I stood up. "I, uh, was up here, on campus, so I thought I'd drop by and say hi. I, well, I left that party early, you know, the night the play opened, so we didn't have a chance to talk."

"I wondered where you went."

"Well, Alec wanted to leave, and you were. . .busy, dancing with the Bir. . .Tom and Randy."

"I guess three people dancing together is weird, but dancing alone is weirder. Come on in, I've got a few minutes before my next class." I followed him into the office and took a chair. He sat down at the desk and put his hands behind his head. "So what can I do for you? Or is this visit strictly social?"

"I just wanted to tell you how much I enjoyed the play." Not a great line, but I'd been practicing it in case I ran into him somewhere and needed an opener.

"Oh, that. Thank God it's over. You have no idea what it's like having to work with amateurs. I'll be glad when I get my masters so I can ditch this town and all this third-rate talent."

"They're not *all* bad, are they? I mean, Kelly, isn't he supposed to be good?"

"*Supposed* to be is right. He's found his niche here. He's about right for this place. How can you stand it in this hick town? Why didn't you leave when you graduated?"

"Well, I never did. I quit school." I wondered if he'd heard the rumors, about me flunking out. When he didn't say anything, I held up the course list. "But I'm planning to go back and finish."

"I'd think so — that degree's gonna be my passport out of here." He looked at his watch. "Look, I'm flattered you came all this way to see me. I don't have time to go out and meet people. I stop in at that dump, the Alamo, once in a while, go to those insipid parties just to make an appearance, you know, in the hopes I'll find *someone* worth my time. Tom and Randy are crazy about me, so I let them drag me out once in a while, but I've got a career to think about." He headed for the door, so I took his cue and stood up. "Keep trying, Joe, I could probably find some time for a guy like you. Sorry, gotta run."

Well, I thought, as I rode down the elevator, this guy wasn't what I'd call a shrinking violet. And he sure wasn't mellow. I'd half expected to hear him say he had to stay exclusive. But he had seemed glad to see me, he'd even encouraged me. And let's face it, there was no one else for me to set my sights on. And he was gorgeous. If not much else.

SCENE V

Pipe Dream

Alec was already home when I got there, and in a surprisingly good mood. "I did see Kelly, after all," he told me. "He was busy, but at least he took a few minutes to talk to me."

"Explaining your good mood?"

"No, it's not that. The play — it's been chosen to compete in a collegiate drama competition. Depending on how they do in the early rounds, they might get to do quite a lot of traveling this summer."

"And you're hoping to go along?"

"You're getting way ahead of me. All I mean is, it'll be a great opportunity for the cast. Tom and Randy will have a ball."

"Oh. So you didn't get anywhere with Kelly after all."

"Joe, he's not interested in me. Period. I'm still waiting for him to just say 'thanks' for the help I gave him. I'm beginning to have my doubts about him, anyway. He's not really that great, not like I once thought."

"Hey, give the guy a break. He's been busy, you said so yourself. Give it a little time. Don't rush it. Get to know him better."

He looked at me suspiciously. "What's gotten into you? That's exactly the advice I gave *you.* What happened this afternoon, when you saw Rob? You did see him, didn't you?"

"Yeah, I saw him. And I think he likes me. I'd say he was very encouraging."

"So what's your next move?"

"Well, I thought you might be able to help me out. I can't just make up reasons to drop in on him. I need an event, an occasion."

"What does that have to do with me?"

"Uh, the occasion I had in mind was a little party."

"Oh, good," he said, throwing out his arms, " 'I need a brand new dress, a fairyland new dress.' "

"Stop singing. I didn't mean *that* kind of party. I was thinking of more like a small, intimate party. A dinner party."

"Just the three of us? 'La, how jolly.' "

"Alec! You have to invite Kelly."

"So that's what you were up to. I don't want to invite Kelly."

"I'm thinking of you, too. Maybe if you get him away from the office, away from the theater, get him to relax. I'll bet he comes to his senses." He sighed. But I could tell he was weakening. "And Kelly and Rob, they get along, don't they?" After all, Rob hadn't actually said he didn't *like* the guy. Besides, Rob and Kelly liking each other wasn't the point. They could put aside their differences for one night. "It would make a perfect foursome. Come on, Alec, what do you say?"

"I don't know. . . ."

"It's really important. How else will I get to know Rob? You want me to get to know him, don't you? You wouldn't want to think I was just interested in his looks, would you?"

He looked at me with his eyes narrowed. "So you want to get to know Rob, eh? You're right, maybe you *should* get to know him better."

"So you'll do it?"

He clasped his hands together and looked up at the

ceiling. "Time for another chorus of 'What I Did for Love,' " he sighed. "OK, I'll do it." I was so happy I grabbed him and gave him a big hug. "Better not do this in front of your new boyfriend," he said with a laugh.

But I didn't care. I'd gone a long time without getting any hugs, and it was, after all, only Alec. I mean, if you can't hug your roommate, who can you hug?

We set the date and got on the phone. I was a little nervous about calling Rob, but he accepted immediately. Alec's cooking, he said, was famous, and he hadn't had a decent meal since he'd hit town.

A dinner party was all it took to cheer Alec up. He had a whole week and a half to plan for it. He spent days thumbing through his enormous collection of cookbooks, trying to decide on a menu. I could tell he was having trouble making up his mind — there was no theme to the snatches of songs I heard coming from the kitchen. He had all the basic food groups covered, and a few more. At first I thought it was going to be poultry, though I had my doubts about the breast of peacock in there with the chicks and ducks and turkey-lurkey. Meat seemed safe, since he sang about nothing more exotic than beefsteak, roast beef, and ham, and the seafood selections were limited to deviled crabs, lobster claws, and clambakes. The vegetables sounded iffy — I mean, were there really songs about turnip greens and rutabagas? Some of his tunes had me more than a little worried — apparently pickled pigs' feet, mozzarella burgers, and roughage had all had their turn on the musical stage, not to mention songs about popping pussies into pies, putting Benzedrine in Ovaltine, and eating octopus in Borneo.

I think we were both relieved when he finally announced the menu, medallions of veal with raspberries from his California *nouvelle* cookbook. Once that was set, he was a whirlwind of activity. Alec's moods were infectious, so I felt increasingly excited as the big night approached. I'd painted such a rosy picture for Alec that all my own reservations about Rob evaporated. I knew that sitting there in the candle glow, drinking good wine and eating his veal, he'd turn out to be a real sweetheart. I was counting on it.

I started daydreaming about him; it seemed to be a habit of mine. I'd noticed in the summer school catalog that he was teaching a course, and I kept thinking what it would be like if I was taking a class myself. I'd have to rearrange my work schedule, maybe even go part-time. But I knew Bud wouldn't give me any trouble. I was doing too good a job. So I pictured myself meeting Rob after class, for lunch, maybe driving out in the country for a picnic. Then, after a great dinner at home with Alec, I'd meet him again for some studying, and after that. . . . I finally felt I had something to look forward to; things started to matter again. And not just going back to school. I attacked my running and workouts with new vigor and determination. The day before the party I got so carried away thinking about Rob that I forgot to raise the weights on the bicep machine and almost punched myself in the face. Rob had great biceps. Finding out about the rest was going to be my summer project. Homework, so to speak. One night my home, one night his. . . .

"Hey, Joe, my man, long time no see."

"Oh, Jerry. Hi."

"Still messing around with this kid stuff, huh? You know, I miss having you as my workout buddy. What do you say?"

"I don't think so, Jer. I like the machines."

"Come on, Joe, it'd be great. And don't think I've forgotten about our little talk, either. I've still got that prospectus to show you." He punched my arm in that playful way of his. "You're not getting any younger, my man."

"Jer?"

"Yeah, Joe?"

"Buzz off."

"Hey, I'm only trying to do you a favor." I went over to the tricep machine and adjusted the seat. He finally got the message and walked off muttering. "Some guys, you want to help 'em out. . . ."

The morning of the dinner Alec was in the kitchen early, pounding the veal and singing at the top of his voice: "What a Night This Is Going to Be," "Tonight," "Everything Beautiful Happens at Night," "Nine O'Clock." I didn't know if he was happy because he was doing what he liked to do best, or if he'd decided that maybe things would work out with Kelly after all. Whatever he was hoping would come of this dinner, it was nothing compared to my expectations.

I went out for an early run, then laid out my clothes for the evening. I'd wondered if velour was still in, but a new catalog I found at the gym assured me it remained a fashion favorite. I had a nice gray velour shirt that made my eyes look bluer, and I figured the soft look would project "cuddly." Rob wouldn't be able to resist.

I had to work that Saturday, but nothing could take my mind off the party. I'd really built this dinner up in my head, thinking about it, imagining the conversation. Kelly would have eyes for Alec, jumping up from the table every few minutes to help in the kitchen. Rob and I would be alone. Our knees would touch and we'd smile, as if it had been an accident. The talk would be clever and witty; I might even tell some of my favorite stories from my days on the farm. But no sheep jokes — this was a sophisticated crowd. The wine would flow, the candle-light would accentuate Rob's cheekbones; the evening might even wind down to a glorious conclusion with Alec and me leading our dates into separate bedrooms. I watched the clock all afternoon, but the hours dragged by.

To make matters worse, Judy seemed especially obnoxious that day, looking at me, starting conversations and not finishing them. Driving me crazy. Finally she cornered me behind the jogging bras.

"You're awfully jumpy today, Joe. Anything wrong?"

"No, things are fine. In fact, you're the one who seems antsy."

"Uh, Joe, I've got to talk to you. It's important. We're off at six, maybe we could go someplace?"

"I can't Judy, not today. I have to get home."

"Just give me a little time. Five minutes."

"Aw, Judy. . . ."

"Two minutes."

It was all I could do to get my window display done that afternoon. I'd begun thinking of the front window as a stage. Instead of putting the mannequins in the usual static poses, I tried to arrange little scenes, maybe even tell a story across the front of the whole store. My special gimmick was to outfit the mannequins in all the latest in sports equipment and clothes, then place them in the most unlikely settings — a garden, a fancy restaurant. It was easy to come up with ideas, all I had to do was listen to the songs Alec sang or glance at a couple of album covers. The windows were starting to attract a lot of attention. Bud loved it; he gave me credit for the increase in business — not to mention a budget to work with. I'd learned to do wonders with *papier-mache.* The displays were fun. I enjoyed letting my imagination run free. I guess I have my own kind of flair, though of course in a masculine sort of way.

I finished a few minutes before six. I hoped to beat it a little early in order to get the jump on Judy. No such luck; she was right on my tail.

"Got time for a cup of coffee, Joe?"

"Look, you said two minutes. So what's up?"

"It's not going to be easy, what I have to say. Can't we at least sit down, grab that bench over there?"

Oh shit. What now? She'd gone off her diet? She couldn't work some new machine at the gym? She was going crazy for wanting me so much? I didn't need anything heavy laid on me, not now. I sat down. At the far end of the bench. "OK, Judy, let's have it."

"Joe, I've lost weight. I can wear clothes I could never wear before. My hair's almost long enough for a perm."

"Judy, you look great. Really. But you don't understand. I'm just not into. . . ." I was on the verge of spilling the beans, spelling it out for her, making the confession I was once so sure she wanted. Anything so I could get home for that dinner. She didn't give me a chance.

"Don't say it, Joe. Don't say anything. It'll only make it harder."

"For Pete's sake, what is it?"

"I've been waiting for you, Joe, improving myself for you. But the thing is. . .I've met someone else."

"What?"

"Someone who likes me the way I am, someone I don't have to try and please. Who really pleases me, if you know what I mean. Don't say anything, Joe, I can see that this is coming as a shock to you, but let me finish. It's too late for us, Joe.Maybe it just wasn't in the cards for you and me. Since Ralph and I. . . ."

"Ralph? The Ralph who works in the store? Who always said you were a . . .uh, a little overweight? That Ralph?"

"I know, I thought he was a creep. But he's made up for all that. He's apologized, told me how wrong he was, how foolish he was to judge me by my looks. And I have you to thank."

"Me?"

"He used you as his example, pointed out how you'd accepted me from the start, talked to me, listened to me. It was because of you he came to see me as a real person. I'm grateful to you, Joe. It seems like everything good that happens to me is your doing."

Uh oh, I thought, wasn't this the way the whole mess started in the first place? "Don't thank me, Judy. It was nothing. Really." She stared down at the pavement. All I could think of was, Ralph? I looked at her. "Ralph?"

"Best of all, he's a great volleyball player. Can you forgive me?"

"Yeah, Judy, I can forgive you. I'm not sure I can forgive Ralph, but you I can definitely forgive."

"Somehow I knew you'd understand. You're a great guy, Joe."

"Anything you say. See ya." I jumped up from the bench and started running up the hill. But I was laughing so hard I got a stitch in my side and had to take a few deep breaths out on the landing. Even so I made it home in record time. I couldn't believe that idiot Ralph! The *SOB* had made a play for Judy behind my back! The nerve! Straight men — I'd never understand them!

SCENE VI

Company

Alec had everything worked out on a schedule. My job, after a shower and change, was to rearrange the living-room furniture and bring out the kitchen table, then set it, complete with candles and the cut flowers Alec had bought on his last trip out to the store. I'd had to practice folding napkins into unusual shapes for one of my window displays, and we agreed that the bird-of-paradise design looked best. Alec turned the burners under all the pots down to low, pulled the foil off the hors d'oeuvres, and at 7:30 we declared everything ready. We sat down and waited for the bell to ring.

By 7:45 I was starved; my stomach was grumbling so loudly I thought the pictures on the wall would tilt. I didn't dare start in on the hors d'oeuvres — they were works of art. Alec had wrapped thin slices of sun-cured Spanish ham around carefully carved melon wedges and arranged them on a platter, with watercress garnish, to look like flowers. They were really beautiful. But untouchable.

After ten more minutes, Alec was pacing. "This may be what they call 'fashionably late' in New York," he muttered, "but I call it 'unfashionably rude.' " I tried to distract myself by checking every few minutes to see if my hair was still perfectly combed.

Kelly arrived first. I'd never seen the guy before, so

I was more than a little surprised. After all that talk about the exciting, dynamic Kelly, I was expecting someone a little more. . .theatrical. This guy looked like any old college professor. Early thirties, with thinning hair, a beard, wire-rimmed glasses. Didn't he even know that square frames were in? Alec introduced us and he shook my hand. The grip spelled trouble. I mean, the guy said "wimp" all over. And this was the man who'd tied Alec up in knots all those weeks? No way, I thought, Alec deserved better than this. But there I was jumping to conclusions again. I'd only just met the guy. He undoubtedly had some hidden charms that would become apparent as the evening progressed. I hoped so, for Alec's sake.

No sooner had Alec poured the champagne than the two of them started right off jabbering about that damned play and the competition it was entered in. Kelly started telling Alec how little he was looking forward to the prospect of traveling.

"A baby-sitter!" he complained. "I didn't get to this point in my life to baby-sit a bunch of kids and ride all over the country in a bus!"

I wondered if Alec was harboring some secret desire to go along, but I hoped not. I wasn't used to living alone, and it had been a long time since I'd been reduced to eating peanut butter.

"Oh, come on, Kelly," Alec protested, trying to calm him down. "It's a feather in your cap that the production was chosen. You should be delighted. It really was good."

"Yes, it was, wasn't it? Not perfect, but good."

"What would you have done differently?"

"It didn't quite come together here and there. And let's face it, it's a dancing show." He lowered his voice. "And frankly, the choreography wasn't all it should have been."

Uh oh, I thought, does this guy know who else is on the guest list? Alec shot me a glance. ''You liked the dancing, didn't you, Joe?''

''Sure. I thought it was great. Considering it was a group of amateurs.''

''If you ask me,'' Kelly answered, ''the biggest amateur in the bunch was Rob. I mean, a year out of college and he thinks he's ready to conquer Broadway. I've been to New York, *I* know what it's like. Sure, Rob has potential, but he's going to need some seasoning before he's close to ready for the big time.''

Then the bell rang. And not, I feared, to save us. Rob came in, and, with a flourish, took off his bronze-colored Spanish officer's coat, revealing an Australian sheepherder's shirt and Tunisian explorer pants, in sand. After he greeted Alec and me, I watched his face to see how he'd react to seeing Kelly, standing in the kitchen door. I expected him to wince or frown. Instead, he brightened.

''Kelly!'' he said, running over with his arms open wide. ''How's the best director this side of Forty-Second Street?''

''Rob, sweetheart! Always delighted to see my favorite choreographer.'' They embraced and kissed. Alec shot me another glance. And I was afraid they wouldn't get along?

''So, Kelly,'' Rob went on, holding Kelly's hand, ''our little production has been singled out for competition. How does it feel to be going on the road?''

''Just marvelous. It'll really get my juices flowing. And what an opportunity for the kids. But I'll be back for the summer series. Don't you worry, you'll still have me barking at you from the back of the theater.''

''I'd be worried if it was anybody *but* you. Now about the summer season . . . have you decided what you're going to do?''

''Grab yourself a glass of this champagne, Robbie,

and I'll tell you all about it.'' Kelly picked up the platter of appetizers I'd been trying hard not to devour and carried it to the coffee table. He and Rob sat down together on the sofa and started to talk, absent-mindedly reaching over to take aim at Alec's carefully arranged platter.

''Alec,'' Rob called, ''do you have any more of these munchies? I'm so hungry even the napkins would taste good.'' They'd finished off the platter, leaving a trail of watercress across the table and onto the rug.

Alec looked annoyed as he took another tray from the refrigerator. ''Well, here goes tomorrow's lunch,'' he whispered, chewing on the inside of his lower lip.

''Can't you just serve the dinner? I wouldn't mind speeding up the schedule a little.''

''The veal needs another few minutes. Besides, let them burn themselves out. Then we can talk about other things.''

Or so we hoped. When Alec finally announced dinner, Kelly put his arm around Rob's shoulder and guided him to the table. They sat down and dug into their poached pears stuffed with crab curry and didn't miss a beat of their conversation. Alec and I stared at our plates, listening to a play-by-play account of the summer theater schedule. We were finished before they'd even mentioned the third play.

''So, Joe,'' Alec said, turning to me, when the veal was finally on the table. ''How was work today? Did you have a preview of the summer selling season?''

''We were standing room only all afternoon. I sold a rowing machine.''

''A rowing machine! How marvelous!'' He waved his hand in an imitation of the gesture Kelly had just used in response to Rob's suggestion of how they ought to stage a particular production number.

''And what's new at the record store?'' I asked Alec,

while Rob and Kelly debated who should get the lead in one of their shows — the talented boy, the cute boy, or the boy who's father ran a string of dinner theaters in Florida?

"Oh, the usual," Alec answered. "Business is flat. Just keeps going around in circles."

We could have taken off our clothes and thrown raspberries at each other, for all Rob and Kelly would have noticed. When Alec reached for the platter of meat and made a move to get up, I was relieved. Anything to get this meal over with sooner.

"Hey," Kelly said, glancing our way for the first time, "don't take that away. There's plenty left."

Alec's mouth tightened and he put the platter down. Hard. Kelly speared a piece of veal on his fork, dribbling drops of raspberry juice on the table cloth.

"Tomorrow's dinner?" I asked Alec. There was no need to whisper. In fact, I almost had to shout to make him hear me. Alec just nodded, his eyes narrow with anger.

He began to clear the dishes from our half of the table. When I got up to help, I accidentally bumped Rob's leg. He gave me a pained look. "Careful, there, Joe, my legs are my tools. I've got a career to think about."

And I'd been waiting for him to talk to me! I suddenly flashed on an image of what he must be like in bed. I could just see it. "Careful there, Joe. Everything from the waist down is off limits. My career, you know." I'll bet he didn't even take off his hand-knit, one-of-a-kind Afghan socks.

By the time we got the rest of the dishes off the table, it was after ten. "Who the fuck invited these people?" Alec asked when we were alone in the kitchen.

"It's just coffee and dessert and we're home free," I answered. I carried in the cups while Alec sliced the pie. He put the plates on the table just as Rob and Kelly began a debate over which of two plays would better end their season.

"It seems to me," Alec said, taking advantage of a brief lull while the other two had their forks in their mouths, "that if you're trying to pick plays that have something in common with each other, you'd be better off —"

Kelly looked up at him where he was standing in the doorway to the kitchen. "Alec," he said, gulping down a mouthful, "I know you have a lot of opinions, but you have to *work* in the theater, professionally, to really understand what this is all about."

The color drained from Alec's face, and his hand tightened around the handle of the knife he'd used on the pie. I jumped up and pulled him into the kitchen.

"Put the knife down, Alec. You're going to hurt yourself." I pried it from his fist and put it in the sink.

"Who the hell does that goddam bastard —?"

I was almost as mad as he was, but my anger gave way to an urge to protect him, to take care of him. It was a funny feeling, something I'd never felt before. Maybe it was just guilt over having made him go through with this dinner party. Or maybe it was more than that. I couldn't say. I put my hand on his arm. "Take it easy, Alec, stay calm. The evening's almost over. The worst is behind us."

"It had better be," he said, between clenched teeth.

We were just about to sit down at the table when there was a loud pounding at the door. Alec and I exchanged "what now?" glances and both went to answer it. If we'd been lucky, it might have been a fireman, telling us the house was burning. Or a team of narcs busting in at the wrong address. Or the bomb squad, warning us to evacuate. But we weren't lucky. It was Harold, and he was hopping mad.

"Alec," he shouted as he barged in. "I've got to talk to you."

"Harold," Alec hissed, "what are you doing here at this hour? Can't you see we have company?"

Harold looked past us to the table, where Rob and

Kelly had shut up long enough to turn and see what was going on. "Harold," Kelly called out, "how's everybody's favorite theater critic tonight?"

"Don't let me bother you, boys," he chirped back. The two at the table resumed their conversation, and Harold turned on Alec. "Will you kindly tell me the meaning of this outrage? What are you trying to do, ruin me?"

"Harold, what on earth are you talking about?"

"It's a little late to play the innocent. Where have you been?"

"Well, let's see if we can't figure this out. You're in my apartment. My guests are having dinner. Someone had to cook that dinner. Where do you think I've been?"

"What I want to know is, why weren't you at the Methodist Church?"

"For starters, I'm not Methodist."

"Stop playing games, Alec. There was a play tonight in the meeting room of the Methodist Church. *Godspell,* remember?"

"Sounds appropriate."

"Why weren't you there? You *said* you'd be there."

"This is the first I've heard of it."

"Alec, I told you about this play weeks ago. You *promised* you'd be there."

"I most certainly did not."

"Did I, or did I not talk to you on the phone three days ago?"

"You did."

"Didn't I say I'd see you this weekend?"

"Yes."

"And didn't *you* say you'd meet me as usual?"

"Yes."

"So?"

"So what? I was talking about the radio show. I

thought you wanted to get together to pick out the songs you were going to use. Like we do every Sunday.''

Before Harold could say anything, Rob called out from the table. ''Harold, why don't you take your coat off, have some coffee? Alec won't mind. We need your advice. We can't decide what play to do, so we might as well ask the guy who knows more about musical comedy than anyone else in town.''

I could try to describe the look on Alec's face when he heard *that* remark, but let's just say I was glad that knife wasn't still in his hand. Even Harold sensed the depth of Alec's anger and took a few steps back. I was about to reach out to grab Alec, but he whirled around and headed for the table with slow, deliberate steps. I didn't know whether to go after him or try to get Harold out the door. But I saw Alec lean over the table and say something about a slight misunderstanding, so I knew he'd managed to control himself. I stood there, watching Harold stew, his arms crossed, his foot tapping.

Then he turned and looked at me. ''What are you smiling about?''

''I'm just glad to see you, Harold.''

He said something that sounded like ''hmph'' and waited for Alec to come back. ''All right, now,'' he said, pointing his finger at Alec's chest, ''this situation isn't hopeless. There's a performance tomorrow night. You can catch that one. It'll make my review a day late, but I'll tell them I got sick, couldn't make the deadline. Be there tomorrow. At eight.''

''Don't be ridiculous, Harold. Write the review yourself. It's not like the show is deep.''

''You don't understand,'' he said, gritting his teeth. ''I missed it.''

''What do you mean, you 'missed' it?''

''I couldn't make it. Something came up.''

"Something like what?"

Harold looked down at his feet and rubbed his shoes together. "This kid . . . . hitchhiking . . . out on the intersate." Then he looked up and shrugged. "For Christ's sake, I was halfway to the city before I realized he wasn't going to play ball. I made it to the theater for the last ten minutes and the curtain call. I was frantic trying to find you. I had to tell a dozen people how much I enjoyed it." Alec and I looked at each other, and all our tension and anger dissolved into laughter. Harold pouted. "It's not funny, Alec. Now you be there!"

I watched Alec out of the corner of my eye, wondering what he'd do next. Now that he'd had a good laugh over Harold's antics, I was afraid he'd cave in under that idiot's bullying. Rob and Kelly were still going strong at the table, having returned to the subject of their show and the upcoming competition. "I knew it was good," I heard Kelly say, "but I didn't realize just *how* good till I read Harold's brilliant review. Harold, at least, is a pro." Alec's jaw tightened; all was not lost.

"I will *not* go to that play, Harold. Write your own damned review. If you missed it tonight, then *you* go back. I've had it." Hooray for Alec! Standing up to the bullies at last! If it wasn't for the other people there, I might even have hugged him.

Harold looked like he'd had the wind knocked out of his sails. "Now, Alec, think what you're saying. You don't really mean it."

"Like hell he doesn't," I chimed in. I didn't want to give Alec a chance to change his mind.

Then Harold turned on me. "Did you put him up to this? What do you know about it, you . . . you . . . Neanderthal!"

"Now Harold," Alec said, "there's no need to resort to name calling."

"All right," he said. "You've had your little laugh. You win; I'll go back tomorrow night. But in the future it's going to be business as usual."

"I meant what I said, Harold. You're on your own."

He got cocky. "Is that so? Fine. Don't you think I can? I did it alone long before I ever met you, and I can do it again. And to think I was doing you a favor. You've seen a lot of fine theater the last couple of years, thanks to me."

"Sure, Harold, you were only doing it for me. I'm truly grateful."

"Don't patronize me, Alec. Don't humor me. I don't have to listen to this from you, or," pointing to me, "the bionic moron over here. I've got my dignity, my self-respect."

I couldn't take it anymore. "Knock it off, Harold," I said, raising my voice to be heard over the noise at the table. "You lost your self-respect the day you offered me ten bucks to suck my dick in the tea room."

Why is is that everyone at a party stops talking at precisely that instant when someone blurts out something he'd rather die than have the other's hear? The silence that fell just before I made my comment was a roar compared to the silence that followed it. Four jaws dropping in unison don't make a sound.

Needless to say, Harold didn't wait to be shown to the door. Rob and Kelly stared into their laps as if they expected to find something in their napkins. I suppose I should have felt humiliated, but for some strange reason, I just didn't care. In fact, I almost felt exhilarated, as if Alec and I had won a victory, together. And seeing Rob and Kelly looking so uncomfortable made me feel even better. So I strode over to the table and sat down, wondering what happened to my slice of rhubarb custard pie.

Alec came out of the kitchen holding my pie and the

coffee pot, his mouth stretched into a big smile. "Well, gang, more coffee anyone?" He might just as well have started singing "The Party's Over." Rob and Kelly sat there, running their forks around their empty plates and looking embarrassed. But I figured, what the hell, the pie looked great. So I started eating while the others watched me out of the corners of their eyes. I wondered if anyone was ever going to say anything.

"This reminds me of that scene in *Wonderful Town*," Alec began cheerily. "You know, where these people are sitting around trying to make conversation. But everything they say falls flat. So finally, Ros Russell, she plays Ruth, the older sister, finally she says, 'I was rereading *Moby Dick* the other day. It's a story about a . . .whale.' Well, of course, that's hardly a conversation starter. . . .Would anyone like to hear a few numbers from *Wonderful Town*?"

Rob and Kelly sank a little lower in their chairs, and I started laughing. Not just a giggle, either — no, I looked around at the scene and gave out with a full-fledged guffaw. Which was too bad, since my mouth was full, and half-chewed custard is not a pretty sight. Rob and Kelly exchanged looks that said "how do we get out of here?" And after a couple more minutes of awkward silence as I dabbed my napkin on my no longer cuddly velour shirt, they made their lame excuses and hurried out the door.

"Well," I said to Alec when we were finally alone, "I sure know how to bring a party to an early end."

"I'd like to think I did my part, too. I hate making a fool of myself if it's not for a good cause. I was on the verge of pouring hot coffee in those two's laps *before* Harold got here; I wouldn't have been able to put up with them for another five minutes."

"So much for our plans to win those two losers. That Rob has got to be the most arrogant SOB I've ever met."

"Yes, I'm afraid he is."

"You already knew that, didn't you? Why didn't you tell me?"

"You were in love with his looks. Would you have believed me?"

"Probably not." I sighed. "I guess I knew what he was like, but I kept making excuses for him. It's this habit of mine. I overlook a guy's bad points; I dream, I fantasize, I imagine that what's inside has to match up with what's outside. You'd think I'd learn, wouldn't you?"

"I was hoping you would. I'd hate to have to keep fixing fancy dinners till you saw the light."

"I'm sorry Kelly didn't work out, either."

He waved his hand. "I gave up on Kelly a long time ago. I just couldn't convince *you* of that. I was impressed because he was a success in the theater. I was flattered, at first, that he listened to what I said. I knew he was using me. Talk about making the same mistake over and over. . . . but you were always after one guy or another, and I needed something to keep me occupied." His voice trailed off, and I wondered what I had to do with it, why he'd care what I was up to. Then he spoke up again. "I'm tired of being used. I've finally learned my lesson."

"Does that mean you were serious, about letting Harold loose, refusing to help him any more?"

"Oh, I was serious all right."

"What changed your mind?"

"You really want to know? I don't have to tell you, I was already working on a mood before he even showed up. I mean, I've spent the last week slaving in that kitchen over a meal worthy of the cover of *Gourmet,* and not *once* did either of those slobs even mention the food, except to demand more. But to listen to Kelly fawn over Harold, the great theater expert, who, I happen to know, Kelly can't even *stand,* all the while knowing, as only I know, that Harold couldn't review his own bowel movement — I mean, I was ready to kill then and there. But that's still not what did it. What really did it, what *finally* did it, was when I came in here to apologize to those slobs for the scene Harold was making, I saw that those two gluttons had not only eaten *their* desserts, they'd eaten *ours,* too. That piece I brought you was the one I'd set aside for tomorrow's late-night snack. But did either one of them compliment the pie? After what I went through to get fresh rhubarb this time of year? So you know what Kelly said to me? 'Alec, this applesauce is a little sour.' *That's* what he said. When I heard that, Harold didn't stand a chance."

So Harold, if he only knew it, was ultimately done in by a rhubarb custard pie. Which seemed, somehow, very appropriate.

SCENE VII

Over Here!

We cleared off the table and piled the dishes in the sink. But neither one of us was in the mood to wash them, so Alec got out the brandy. "Did Harold really offer you money in the tea room?" he asked, handing me a glass.

"He really did. I ran out on him, but I was scared to death he'd seen me. After that, it was like waiting for the other shoe to drop. For a while I was afraid I might actually have to be nice to him."

"Hard cash isn't so bad. I sold myself for free theater tickets."

"Admit it, Alec, you enjoyed writing those reviews. You liked seeing your stuff in print, even if someone else's name was on it."

"I guess so."

"It's too bad that part of it will have to end."

"Maybe. Maybe not."

"Alec, what are you up to now?"

"What the hell, it's not like we have any secrets. See, the real reason I agreed to help him out was because he was having trouble up at the university. Something about a promotion. All he had going for him was those reviews. But the editor of the paper wasn't happy with Harold's stuff. Threatened to let him go. So I stepped in, and Harold got his promotion. But he knows that without me, his writing will be as bad as it used to be. So before the editor threatens to let him go again, I think he'll be willing to deal. In fact, I think he'll be willing to suggest that he have an assistant, one who'll get to sign his own name to the reviews."

"Do you really think he'd do that?"

He grinned at me. "If he doesn't, he loses the radio show, too. He can think about that tomorrow, when he's up at the station trying to put a program together on his own. Oh, I won't be greedy. I'll still lend him a hand, let him sign his own name when it's a big road show in the city. But I'll get my share of the local stuff. Like in the song 'Just the Crust,' where he says he'd be happy with the crumbs left on the plate."

He leaned over to refill my glass. "Alec, you're something else. I'm proud of you. And even with those idiots, the dinner was fabulous." I could see he was flustered, he almost spilled the brandy. And he blushed. He looked kind of cute, with his face all red, and that same funny urge came over me, to take care of him. So I put my arm around his bony shoulder. Only it didn't feel bony. Now I was sure something was up. "Alec, have you been putting on weight?"

"Who, me?"

"I think all that tasting in the kitchen has caught up with you." I leaned back and took a good look at him. "You have gained weight. You're not nearly as skinny as you used to be."

He blushed again. "I've been working out."

"What? Get off it!"

"No, it's true. Up on campus. Former students are allowed to use the gym. I've been going up there for a couple of months now."

"Why didn't you tell me? I could've helped you out."

"I was embarrassed. At first I didn't believe it would really make a difference, then I wanted to see how long it would take you to notice. And besides, I know you like to use the machines. I wanted fast results, so I've been lifting. You know, free weights. Flies, squats, the works. You ought to try it, you can really build yourself up."

I couldn't believe what I was hearing. "Come over here." I felt his arms, his back, put my hands on his chest. "By God, Alec, you've got muscles! I can't believe it! You're just one surprise after another today. What made you start exercising?"

"What do you think? You, of course. I mean, a guy can't live around physical perfection all these months and not start feeling a little. . . inadequate. You were my inspiration."

So he'd done it because of me. I was confused, not to say a little overwhelmed. To think someone would want to change himself because of me. God knows, Tony never had. Sure, I was willing to change when I started lifting with Jerry, but that was only because I wanted to get into those Italian racing pants of his. And Judy, she'd started to improve herself for my sake, but she just wanted to get into *my* pants. But Alec, he didn't have any ideas like that. Did he? I'd have known. After all, I was very perceptive when it came to people. Wasn't I? Sure, he made jokes about my behind, but those were just jokes, weren't they? I had to admit he'd been acting weird lately, those little fits of what seemed like jealousy, that remark about wanting to keep busy because I was pursuing other guys. But he couldn't be in love with me. It wasn't possible. We were too different. After all, we fought half the time. OK, so we always made up, and he *was* my best friend, and we did feel comfortable with each other, confide in one another. That's it, we were just good friends. But even so, for Alec to change himself so drastically, because of me. . . . Here it came again, the urge to protect him, take care of him. Why not, that's what friends are for, isn't it? The least I could do was to repay this gesture.

"Alec, I have a favor to ask."

"Do I have to cook anything?"

"No," I laughed, "just give me some advice. See, I've decided to go back to school this summer, and I need you to help me pick my courses."

"Me? You want me to help?"

"Who else? I won't find anyone smarter than you, will I? You might say that you're *my* inspiration."

He was so pleased, he leaned over and hugged me. I hugged him right back. And while I was at it, I felt around to see how his lats and obliques were progressing. He wasn't at the point where we could start trading clothes, but he was on his way. After all, it doesn't matter where you start — it's where you finish that counts. Which is a song cue if ever I heard one.

SCENE VIII

They're Playing Our Song

I woke up the next morning feeling good. Once I took a few minutes to remember what had happened the night before, I realized I had no right to feel good. I *should* have felt awful. The man of my dreams turned out to be a Class A asshole, and I'd made a complete fool of myself not only in front of him, but also in front of Harold, who up until last night I thought had Class A assholedom locked up all to himself. Not to mention Kelly, who, from the little I saw, could probably have made it a three-way tie. So why was I so chipper? Was it because Alec had stood up to Harold, finally put him in his place? Or was it the way he went on with the dinner as if nothing had happened, just to try and put me at ease? Or was it because he admitted he'd started working out, with me as his inspiration? I lay there for a while, smiling to myself, absent-mindedly toying with my cock until I decided it might need my full attention. Funny, thinking about Alec had never had that effect on me before.

But the smell of French toast was wafting in from the kitchen and the sound of Alec banging around, looking for his omelet pan no doubt, made my stomach demand satisfaction first. There'd be time for other organs later.

"I couldn't move the table back into the kitchen by myself," Alec said, as we maneuvered it through the doorway from the living room. "You must be strong as a horse. I respect that more, since I've been going to the gym myself. It's taken you a lot of work to get where you are."

"Anyone can do it," I told him, trying not to act too pleased. 'Now you ought to start running with me."

"You mean it?"

"Sure. It's good exercise. You know, for the cardiovascular system. Besides, it's better when you do it with someone. Why not?"

"But people would see us. Together."

"So?"

"Nothing." He turned away. But I could see he was smiling. "I'll think about it. I'd have to start slowly."

"That's OK. Everybody does. But one thing — no more surprises. It's bad enough you started working out without telling me. Don't let me catch you buying your running shoes from anyone else."

"Yes sir, coach!"

We had our breakfast, then I sat down to relax with the paper. I was thinking about making another pot of coffee, but the box of filters was empty, and I didn't know where he kept the new one. He didn't answer when I called to him, so I stuck my head through his bedroom door. I found him standing at the open window, his elbows on the sill, staring out.

"Anything wrong, Alec? You're not upset about last night, are you?"

He turned and looked at me. "It was a nightmare in every way." Then, launching himself into a sweet soprano, " 'But together, you and I, will laugh at last night some day.' "

Which I took to mean he wasn't upset. I went over to the window and wedged myself in beside him. It was a warm day. The sun was just coming up over the roof and there was a slight breeze. The kind of day when you don't think anything can go wrong. "So what are you thinking about?"

"The yard," he said, looking down. "It's time to plan a garden. The landlord lets me plant a few vegetables in the summer."

I studied the narrow strip of dirt and weeds behind the house. "Down there?"

"It's all I've got. I don't do much. Some tomato plants. Peppers, eggplant. Zucchini grows anywhere. I hope you like ratatouille."

"Whatever it is, I'm sure I'll like it. But what about some corn? I haven't had a good ear of corn since I left home."

"I don't think there's enough room down there for corn."

"Sure there is. Right along the fence."

"That's where the tomatoes go."

"No, they should go on the other side, by the gate. If you cut that lilac back, they'd get sun all day. Tomatoes need a lot of sun. And around the side, by the basement door, that would be a perfect spot for a compost heap."

He looked at me. "Compost heap? How do you know about all this?"

"Hey, I'm a farm boy, remember? Who do you think helped grandma plant her kitchen garden every summer? Who do you think took a blue ribbon at the county fair when he was only eleven?"

"You? For what?"

"Biggest damn cucumber you ever saw."

He giggled. "At eleven? Precocious little brat, weren't you?"

"I knew what I liked." He slapped my wrist. "But really, Alec, with a little planning, we could grow a lot down there."

"It would take hard work."

"No sweat. We'd just have to clear the weeds out."

"Some of those dandelions are as old as you are.

Ever try to get rid of dandelions. They have huge taproots. Leave in one little piece and the damn thing comes back stronger than ever. They can really take over."

I nudged him with my hip. "Oh, come on, what are a few dandelions to a couple of bodybuilders like us?"

"Speak for yourself," he said, looking down at his skinny arm pressed against mine.

"Lighten up, Alec. We both like to garden. We have something in common after all."

"Maybe."

"What do you mean, maybe? What's bothering you?"

He pointed down at the ground. "That. A piddling weed patch. Some day I'm going to have a lot of space. I'll grow every vegetable you can think of. And put them up for winter. And I'll have an old house with a big cool basement that I'll fill with stuff I've canned. Jam, preserves. And a root celler. I even know where it's going to be, out south of town, you know, where the highway crosses the railroad tracks and there are lots of old brick houses?"

"Why some day? Why not now?"

"Can't afford it."

"Sure you can. You're making good money. And some of those old places need work. You could probably pick one up cheap. We could fix it up."

"You're a carpenter, too? And a plumber?"

"Don't be such a downer. We could do a lot of it ourselves. And I can afford to pay more than the rent on this place costs me. I could run out that way a couple of mornings and see what's available." I leaned my shoulder into his and pressed him against the window frame. "What do you say?" He sighed. "Come on Alec, it wouldn't hurt to look. You could check the listings in the paper." He sighed again, a long, weary sigh. "Why not?"

"For one thing, you keep saying 'we.' "

"Sure. You don't want to live alone, do you?"

''I thought you were planning to move out. As soon as you could.''

''Well, I suppose I might have said something to that effect. That was before.''

''Before what? Before Rob? Before that guy at the gym you liked? Before the next pretty face you get a crush on?'' Uh oh, he was going weird again.

''Hey, I know better now. I'm not about to rush into anything.'' I put my hand on his shoulder. ''What do you say? Let's have a look in the paper.''

He leaned his head against my cheek. ''Oh, what the hell, it doesn't hurt to look.'' So he turned away from the window and went to get the real estate pages. Leaving me to wonder why I'd gotten a hard-on.

SCENE IX

Bells Are Ringing

I made the second pot of coffee while Alec busied himself with the "Homes for sale" pages of the newspaper. He read and circled and made big Xs, all the while singing a medley that painted a picture of domestic bliss: "Welcome Home," "The Only Home I Know," "You've Come Home," "We're Home." I knew he was really getting into it, with "Plant a Radish" and "Make Our Garden Grow," and afraid he was getting carried away with "How Do You Raise a Barn?" But I just leaned back and smiled. That was how Sunday afternoons should be — a hot cup of coffee, a newspaper, and Alec in a good enough mood that I was sure he'd be inspired come dinner time.

A little while later, when the phone rang, my first guess would have been Harold, calling to patch things up with Alec. But Alec had told me Harold would need a couple of days to let his pride settle, especially since he had to go back and see the play again that he'd missed. So it must have been one of the Birdies. Alec reached for the phone automatically. It was never for me.

Except that time. He nodded at me and held out the receiver. Then he sat back down at the kitchen table and lowered his head over the paper. No one ever called me. I figured it must be something about work, maybe Judy wanting me to trade shifts with her so she and Ralph could go and do whatever it was they did together. I even thought it might be Jerry, tracking me down to make one last stab at raiding my checkbook. "Hello?"

"Hello, Joe."

"Who is this?"

"It's me, Joe." A pause while I tried to place the familiar-sounding voice. "Tony."

I was remarkably calm, I thought, considering this was the man who turned my life upside down the day we met, shook it hard enough that I had to get out, then came close to blowing it up altogether when I learned the truth about him. What was there left for him to do now? I carried the phone to the far end of the room and sank into a chair. For some reason, I didn't want Alec to hear my conversation.

"How ya doin', Joe?"

"I'm OK," I said, my voice low. "How'd you know where I was?"

"You left me the number, remember? Besides, I asked around."

"Around? Where are you?"

"Here. In town." Silence. "So what do you say?"

"About what?"

"About us. You know, gettin' together, maybe for a drink, some laughs, whatever."

"I don't think so, Tony."

"Why not? For old times' sake?"

"No. I don't think it would be a good idea. It's over and done with."

"Who says no? I just thought if we saw each other. . . ."

"Forget it."

Another pause. Then that voice. The bedroom voice. The I-can-make-you-do-whatever-I-say voice. "Don't you miss me, Joe? Just a little? Remember how good it was. I sure miss you."

"You should have thought of that before. A long time ago."

"Hey, man, I'm sorry about all that. You were right. I didn't have my head on straight."

"What are you doing back in town?"

"I, uh, I'm looking for work. Maybe my old job, you know, at the restaurant? I talked to them yesterday. It's as good as settled. So you see, it'd be just like you wanted, I'd be working steady, waiting tables."

"What happened to the job in the city?"

"That? Oh, you know how it is, I got tired of all that crap. There's a lot of turnover in that business. You know, they, uh, they like to have new faces." So he was danced out, was he? Superman had his wings clipped, and now all he could do was crawl. Old meat. "Joe?"

"Yeah?"

"I want you back. Do you remember how it was? Think about it, about the two if us, in bed. My tongue is doing a quick once-over of your ear. Now it's moving around, to the back of your neck. Remember how you used to like that? I'm thinking about it now, Joe. And I'm getting hard. Aren't you?"

Yes. Now I was all mixed up. In just a couple of hours *60 Minutes* would be coming on. Tony would be getting worked up. Turning all red. Turning me on. And then . . . then I remembered Tony the Tunnel.

"You're a health risk, Tony. You're bad for my mental health and a threat to my physical health. Especially now, after all those months messing around in the city."

"Hey, you want a certificate, I'll get one. I'll take the test. Whatever you say. I've changed, Joe. Really. I'll do whatever you want."

These were words I'd never heard from Tony before. I was afraid I was going to give in. I needed something to concentrate on, to help me put my thoughts together.

I looked into the kitchen. Alec wasn't at the table. I picked up the phone and crossed the living room. I noticed the newspaper he'd been reading, the real estate section, sticking up out of the trash can. Then I saw him standing at the sink. His head was down, and he kept raising the backs of his hands to his eyes. He didn't know I was watching him. Even if he hadn't heard every word I'd said, he must have known who I was talking to. And he probably assumed I'd walk out on him, after all the plans we'd been making, that I'd go running right back to Tony. He sure seemed upset. Then it came over me again, that urge to protect him. And *that* made me even more confused.

And suddenly it occurred to me that Tony was like a dandelion — a piece of his taproot had stayed inside of me. And if I let that little piece take hold, it would grow back stronger than ever. And take me over. Dandelions might be pretty, but they were weeds. Grandma used to say that dandelions in the pasture gave the milk an off-taste. And like Alec had told me, they sure were hard to get rid of.

"Forget it, Tony, it's over."

"But Joe —"

"I mean it. We're through." I saw Alec glance my way. "I like it where I am."

"Sure, Joe, there's no hurry. Think it over. You don't have to decide anything right now. You can reach me at the restaurant. Nick, the bartender, he'll know where to find me."

I'll just bet, I thought. "Goodbye, Tony." I hung up.

I went into the kitchen and stood behind Alec at the sink. "I suppose you know what that was all about." He nodded. Then he sniffed and wiped his nose on a paper towel. "Is anything wrong?"

He shook his head. "I was slicing onions, that's all."

I put my hands on his shoulders and looked into the sink. He'd been washing the raspberries he'd managed to set aside from the night before. "Those are mighty small onions.

Funny color, too." He shrugged. I tried to get him to turn around, but he pulled out of my grip and held onto the edge of the sink. It was the first time I'd ever seen him with all his defenses down. I knew now how he felt about me. For that matter, how I felt about him. "Come on, Alec," I whispered in his ear, "don't you want to sing me a song?" He shook his head again. "OK, then I guess I'll be going out for a while."

He whirled around and faced me. His eyes were red and there was a look of near-panic on his face. "Where?"

"To the store. If those are onions, we're going to need some raspberries, aren't we?"

His eyes welled up again, so I took him in my arms and held him. And I'll be darned if I didn't get another hard-on. It was time to do something about this. So I held him closer.

Alec always was a smart guy. It didn't take him long to get the message.

FINALE

"So how about it, Alec, can we take the newspaper out of the trash and start looking again?"

"Still have your heart set on growing the world's biggest cucumber?"

"I think I'm looking at it right now."

"Don't be gross," he said, throwing a pillow over my head. He kneeled beside me, threw out his arms and started to sing. " 'You know how I am, I get embarrassed.' "

"That'll be the day," I laughed, pulling him down onto the bed.

He propped himself up on one elbow and ran his finger around my navel. "It's funny, the way things turned out. I mean, who ever dreamed my life would end up like a musical? But it's just like the boy and girl in *The Fantasticks.* Or Ann and Kipps in *Half a Sixpence.* Or Lizzie and File, Molly Brown and —"

"Alec, I haven't seen any of those shows. What are you talking about?"

"It's really the biggest cliche of all. You go your own way, see a little of life. Of love. Suffer a few defeats. Then realize that the person you love is the one who was waiting at home all along."

"Sometimes it takes time for things to sort themselves out."

"And many a show has run into second act problems trying to figure out how. It sure took us long enough. But in the end you realized the truth in that old saying, 'The fattest rabbit hides in the hunter's own cabbage patch.' "

"Don't tell me — you got that from your grandmother!"

"What grandmother? I read it in some old cookbook. The only advice my grandmother ever gave me was, 'If you've got it, flaunt it.' "

"I have a feeling your grandmother was a lot more interesting than mine. Does that mean I can keep wearing the little blue running shorts?"

"As long as I'm running along next to you, why not? That's show biz."

"As Roxie Hart would say."

He smiled at me, then nibbled my ear. "You know, Joe, there may be hope for you yet. Can you sing harmony?"

I pulled him toward me. "Oh, Alec, you really are *impossible!*"

The author would like to thank all those companies and their representatives who helped in securing permission to quote from the following:

MISTER CELLOPHANE by Fred Ebb & John Kander
Copyright © 1975 by Kander-Ebb Inc., & UNICHAPPELL MUSIC INC.
All Rights Administered by UNICHAPPELL MUSIC INC.
International Copyright Secured ALL RIGHTS RESERVED Used by permission

IT ISN'T ENOUGH from the Musical Production "THE ROAR OF THE GREASEPAINT – The Smell of the Crowd"
Words and Music by Leslie Bricusse and Anthony Newley
© Copyright 1965 Concord Music Ltd., London, England
TRO – Musical Comedy Productions, Inc., New York, controls all publication rights for the U.S.A. and Canada Used by permission

STEP TO THE REAR Composer: Elmer Bernstein & Carolyn Leigh
Copyright: © 1967 By Carolyn Leigh & Elmer Bernstein
All Rights Controlled by CARAVAN MUSIC, INC., 729 7th Avenue, NY, NY
International Copyright Secured Made in USA All Rights Reserved
Used by Permission

HAPPINESS IS A THING CALLED JOE Composer: E.Y. Harburg & Harold Arlen
Copyright: © 1942 Renewed 1970 METRO-GOLDWYN MAYER, INC.
Rights Assigned to SBK CATALOGUE PARTNERSHIP
All Rights Controlled and Administered by SBK FEIST CATALOG INC.
All Rights Reserved International Copyright Secured Used by permission

WITHOUT ME (John Kander, Fred Ebb)
© 1967 – ALLEY MUSIC CORP. and TRIO MUSIC CO., INC.
Used by permission All rights reserved

DEAR FRIEND (Sheldon Harnick, Jerry Bock)
© 1963 – ALLEY MUSIC CORP. and TRIO MUSIC CO., INC.
Used by permission All rights reserved

THE WOMAN FOR THE MAN WHO HAS EVERYTHING
Copyrighted 1966 Lee Adams and Charles Strouse
Used with permission All Rights Protected

OOH, DO YOU LOVE YOU
Copyrighted 1966 Lee Adams and Charles Strouse
Used with permission All Rights Protected

YOU'VE GOT POSSIBILITIES
Copyrighted 1966 Lee Adams and Charles Strouse
Used with permission All Rights Protected

I GET EMBARRASSED by Bob Merrill
© 1957 Golden Bell Songs
All Rights Reserved Used by permission

I CAN COOK TOO by Leonard Bernstein, Betty Comden and Adolph Green
© 1944 Warner Bros. Inc. (Renewed) All Rights Reserved Used by permission

YA GOT ME by Leonard Bernstein, Betty Comden and Adolph Green
© 1945 Warner Bros. Inc. (Renewed) All Rights Reserved Used by permission

Joe was into running, the gym, big pecs, you name it; if it was really macho, Joe was for it.

Alec loved musicals, the theater, and cooking; some of the meekest men in town were his dear friends.

But then Joe came to rent a room in Alec's apartment, just for a few days, or maybe weeks, till he and his lover made up and he could go back home to Tony.

Two men, opposite in every way, learn how to respect each other, to find tolerance for faults, to appreciate the best in the other man. Each has laughs—and tears—along this road of discovery about each other . . . and about themselves, in this warm story of friendship.

The critics rave about his first book: "Larry Howard treats us here to some very fine craftsmanship."—Ken Kildore

"(His) book is extremely well written. Never dragging, the plot aids Howard in developing characters who are not only complex, but real."—Good Times!, Columbus, Ohio

Larry Howard, like Alec, has an extensive collection of Broadway cast albums, and, like Joe, is "into physical fitness." Before he turned to writing fiction, he taught in several western universities. He was educated in his native New York State, but now makes northern Nevada his home.